DEAR GRANDCHILD

Laurence Thomas

DEDICATION

Dedicated to Keni B.
You helped me get through a dark time
allowing me to work through this project, and I appreciate you so much.

CONTENTS

CHAPTER 1

WINTER TALES

"The meeting is set for Thursday?" I asked for confirmation.

"It is."

"Well, at least the leaders of the lower classes did not decide to meet today."

"It's a revolution. Revolution without a doubt!" Damian exclaimed or explained while considering why this was an unusually busy day. So much to plan.

"Well... Be that as it may, it's the holidays. I am with my grandchildren today, and JW., I need you to make sure that we are not disturbed for the rest of the day. You got that?"

"Understood," JW obliged.

Damian walks down the hallway to meet his family. This always put a smile on his face as he felt proud of his ability to support them and for the strides they all made as a result of Damian's tireless efforts and the world he created for them. In a spacious family room with over 1000 square feet of warmth, Damian joined his grandchildren.

This was a massive room with two double-sided fireplaces, three huge sectionals, ten overstuffed chairs that double as beds for those times when the entire family got together (not that the ten bedrooms were not enough accommodation), several beautiful coffee-styled tables and an assortment of throw rugs, stools, artwork, books, and always enough love to be inviting to anyone with breath because this room would truly take one's breath away.

This is where everyone could relax. As Damian entered the room, he lovingly eyed his 9 grandchildren. They ranged in age from 18 down to 7 years old. Two sets of twins! All remarkably close, too. That was a strength of this family. Their closeness allowed them to always move forward.

They met each month and would talk, listen, exchange ideas, eat, laugh, and have a wonderful time together. Damian always believed that the children are our future and that they must be trained correctly so they will know what to do when they reach the Age of Responsibility.

This is one of the things Damian discussed with JW on numerous occasions. They agreed that a good name is better than all the riches in the world.

Today, Damian wanted to tell his grandchildren a story. A true story and an insight into their upcoming responsibilities and one that would help them understand the importance of a good name. Damian was painfully aware of what is often called 'Generational Curses.' These are where a man or woman does bad acts. Acts that are neither moral, ethical, nor righteous. Sometimes they may repent, and other times, they do not. When they do not repent, the 'curse' is in place, and generations to come suffer because of the lack of repenting. Damian believed that spirituality, faith, and belief in The Higher Power would be critical in the battle against these curses. We may not be aware of our ancestors' transgressions, but that will not stop the fate that awaits. Can one truly break generational curses? Most say emphatically: NO. But Damian was determined to make a difference in his grandchildren's lives. Damian hoped that, at a minimum, they would break the curses for their progeny. That maybe their actions will be pure enough to avoid future imprecations. He was determined to regularly talk with his grandchildren about the events in the world and how to deal with them. All while maintaining an instructive tone. A tone where he could use their respect and trust for him to gird them with the knowledge to prepare for, as much as possible, whatever they faced. They would soon be able to establish good names for themselves and be armed to recognize the generational curses and meet them head-on.

Damian passionately believed that one is obligated to let their children know where they come from and where they can go. Inspiration, if you will. A seemingly lost art. An art that not only serves to inform, arm and gird, but art that leads to perpetuating family traditions, values, and potentials. Something to which Damian was completely devoted.

Looking over his grand group, Damian could not help but swell up in pride. And, thinking that he wanted nothing but the best for his grandchildren and knew it was up to him, like all grandfathers and fathers and protectors, to help each know their potential.

Damian walked up to his gifted gang and hugged each one, putting 500 credits into the device held in each grandchild's hand.

"Thank you so much, grandfather," beams Myell. I know just what to do with this".

"You better hold on to it," adds Rahij.

"No, invest it!" chimes Damian III or D3 as he is called by friends and family. "And I have the perfect

investment for you".

Everybody laughs.

After he bestows upon, greets, hugs, and kisses them all, he bids them to all sit. They notice 9 of the overstuffed chairs are arranged in a campfire-like-configuration and as they near their seats, their anticipation immediately skyrockets as they know they are in for one of Grandfather's wonderful winter tales.

Sure, they enjoyed the other gatherings where they played games and discussed different topics that ranged from whether it is right to die for something you honestly believe in, even if that thing is not accepted by many others, to, should we help everybody, even the Dregs, and Wantos.

Grim enough conversation for children, but these were no ordinary children. These were Damian's grandchildren. Born of privilege and protected from the ills of what was a daily occurrence in the world. The strife, the hunger and searching, the deceptions, the killings, the same hurt, harm, and danger he had now dedicated his life to fighting.

They loved his stories, and they loved and greatly respected him. Noticing the excitement on their faces, the Old Patriarch sat in the tenth chair, positioned in front of them all, and began to tell them a different kind of story. This one would help prepare them for the days and months, and years to come.

"You know, guys, when I was younger, I remember we children could not wait to join the fun enjoyed by our elders during the winter holidays. Sure, we had our own entertainment, but there was nothing like the fun the grown-ups seemed to always have. It was a special time that included plenty of food, drink, music, games, love, and laughter."

Now, when I say the family gathering of the year, I mean a *huge* event. It was the event that everyone made time for, regardless of their business. It was the place of acceptance. It was the place where all that mattered was the love between the family members, where we all forgot all quarrels, all arguments, and just gathered together to celebrate being a family.

Grandmommy, as she was affectionately known, would go all out with the décor. She was an amazing hostess who poured love and comfort into the food she made, the sofas she set, in every little detail she touched.

Continuous music accompanied the aroma of cinnamon, and it would be fair to say that the winter party appealed to all five of our senses to instill the best memories in our minds.

You know what was more fun than all this? The card games! There was a very crazy game in which the family members would constantly be shouting at each other. Still, all those yells were accompanied by hysterical laughter and ear-wide smiles.

That game taught me one thing: You cannot always gauge a person's mood by their words, but you can, at most times, by their eyes.

You have no idea how badly I wanted to just grow up, reach 'the age,' and join in on this particular game. That was the first thing I wanted to do at the main party. Now, I am a master at the game, but folks don't like to play with me because they think I cheat." "Grandfather, how could they think that?" Well, I always seem to get the perfect hands, and folks say I put cards in the hand I want them in. Ridiculous, I know! The entire time he spoke, he had a deck of cards in his hands, shuffling them vigorously and revealing the same card on the top no matter how much he rearranged the cards.

Dear grandchildren, I have a particularly important thing to tell you. It is something that my grandfather told me, and I now pass it on to you as a sort of hereditary gift. Each of you will get a special phrase when you are aged 17, and then you will have one year before you reach adulthood to show what you learned from that phrase.

As for me, my special phrase was given by my grandfather when he told me to look at a man's eyes to understand him. He then told me my phrase, "The eyes are the window to the soul," he told me. "You know what I did? I took that phrase to heart and kept it with me not only through to the next year but through life.

Similarly, you know my brother. His special phrase at 17 was Thoreau's: 'Nothing great was ever achieved without enthusiasm,' and boy, is he, one enthusiastic dude! He always has an upbeat attitude and is a cheerful man. It is infectious too. Name one time when you were ever sad around Uncle Arctay. Go ahead; I will wait. This little tradition is one thing that kept an interesting bond between us and between our generations.

"Grandfather, did Grandmommy have a special phrase, too?"

Why, yes, of course! Her special phrase was "Follow your soul – it knows its way," and boy, did she follow her soul a lot! The group of grandchildren laughed.

Your grandmother Rose was a very brave woman. It has not been long now, but you should still have memories of her before she left this world, my dear grandchildren, but she loved you all dearly and would have been the best grandmommy ever, if only... Damian remembers her and pauses.

"Tell us about her, Grandfather. What was the story of her special phrase?"

Do you guys know how I met your grandmother, children?

The grandchildren looked sideways at each other to see if anyone knew anything about it. I laughed.

Well, we used to be neighbors. We were teenagers when she had moved to our neighborhood, and I was her first friend there. Luckily, our parents got along really well and soon became best friends. In fact, our parents became so close that our family traditions were soon picked up by their family, too.

"Wow, that sounds so cute," Elihu giggled.

Yeah… Our parents were best friends, but your grandmommy and I were always fighting. I made her cry when we used to play, and she would piss me off in every way! But, well, like Tom and Jerry, we both knew that we made each other miserable because we loved each other.

"So, grandfather, why would you make her cry if you loved her?"

Because I was a kid and was too young to know that I loved her, but, hear this: I was the one who made her cry, but my entire day would be spent sulking in corners because I hated seeing her cry. I was a stupid kid, guys! Yet, as time passed and as we grew into adults together, Rose and I   understood how we felt about each other, and that is the story of how we met! We didn't marry right away, but we still always knew.

Now, to talk about how she got her special phrase... I was a year older than her, so I had gotten my special phrase first because obviously, I turned 17 first. Eventually, as she saw how exciting it was for me to have this phrase and work on it, she started nudging her parents, too, to start this Holiday tradition.

One year later, on the eve of the big Holiday, she came running across the street to tell me that she had gotten her special phrase, too, and not just her, but her cousins who were between the ages of 17-20 had gotten theirs, too. So, in a way, I had extended our family traditions to her family before we had even gotten married!

As you guys know, your grandmommy was such a lively and soulful person. She was always a ray of sunshine regardless of where she was or who she was with. She turned our house into a home and always welcomed you all, your parents, and any kind face she met, with warm pies and freshly baked cookies.

"You know, I believe that her special phrase shaped the way she went through life. Her decisional strategies, her thinking style, and the ways she expressed love... it was all based on her phrase. She always allowed herself to be guided by her soul and intuition instead of logic and facts. And I loved her so much for that." He says mistily.

"Think from your heart instead of your head... Right?" Nubia asked giddily, smiling from ear to ear as her eyes shone just like her grandmother's.

Exactly, my dear. But again, make sure your heart is pure and free from evil thoughts.

Now, let's talk about you, children. Show of hands, who has gotten their special phrases yet? I believe D3 got his...

"Yes, grandfather! I got mine just recently." He responded excitedly, feeling special for standing out from the group of grandchildren. He was the only one who had gotten his special phrase so far. The rest were too young for it at the time.

"Well, what is it? What is your phrase?"

"I never lose. I either win, or I learn. That's my phrase." He said."Wonderful! That's a wonderful phrase. And what have you understood from this young man?"

D3 paused for a while, thinking of an answer that would make him sound wise as he was the eldest among the group of grandchildren. And, then he responded, "My father gave me this phrase, grandfather. And he explained that every experience is a valuable one and that you always learn from your experiences even if you fail at something."

That is true, my dear grandchildren, and an especially important lesson. I can tell you from my experience that no one always wins, and no one always loses. In every venture that you take up, you have to give your best efforts, but efforts alone do not determine victory. More often than not, your efforts need the support of fate in order to give you success.

My dear kids, life is full of tests and experiences. Sometimes, you will feel lost and scared to take a step, but other times, you might feel thrilled and enthusiastic. In both cases, you must not back off and give up, but instead, work as hard as you can towards achieving your goals. When you do your best, and with the best of intentions, then fate is likely to turn your way, too.

There is this novel that was immensely popular among the youth in my days. It had an incredibly beautiful quote repeated several times in the book that said:

"When you truly want something, the whole universe conspires in helping you achieve it." – Paulo Coelho

"Wow, Grandpa. That is a genuinely nice concept." One of the grandchildren responded with bright twinkling eyes.

Indeed... So, D3, tell us, what did you take away from your special phrase? How have you applied it to your life so far?

"Well, grandfather... It has been only some time since I got this, so I have not had much time yet to work on this phrase. But, I should tell you," D3 continued, thinking as he spoke, "that this phrase had come to my mind while I was learning how to skate. Just a few days ago, my friends and I planned to go skating. I had never skated before, but I wanted to take it on as a challenge. I borrowed a pair of skating shoes from a friend of mine and went to a pond in the south acreage nearby with the group."

The other grandchildren looked at Damian III, interested and invested in his story.

He went on, "I tried to skate several times. When I had put on those shoes and looked at my friends going around the rink so smoothly, they made it look so easy. I thought I could do it in one try because it did not seem like a big deal, but when I tried standing up with the shoes on, I couldn't."

I smiled, watching Damian III go on, proudly telling his struggle story.

"Oh, what happened then?" Arlisha squeaked curiously. D3 was enjoying the attention, too. He was intentionally adding dramatic pauses to make the other children ask him for more.

"Well, I kept trying to get up, and my friends started laughing at me, too, when they saw that I kept falling. But then, instead of feeling like a total failure, I found the courage to keep trying until I could do it.

"Well... long story short: all I could manage that day was to stand with the skating shoes. I never even made it into the rink that day, but instead of coming home feeling like a loser, I came home feeling glad that I had at least learned to stand and stay up while wearing skating shoes…."

"That's it?" One of the twins asked, disappointed. "That's your big win?"

"No, honey, no," I stopped her. "That was not a win. But, because he did not win, he had two options. He could either take it as a failure, feel like a loser, and give up on trying to learn skating, or he could figure out what he learned from failing that day so that he could use that knowledge to further his learning and practice the next time. Isn't that right, D3?"

"Yes, grandfather." Damian III nodded, glad that he was being supported. "That is exactly how I thought that day. I realized that winning or losing is a mindset – if I took that day as a failure, I would not have gone for another practice. Eventually, little by little, I have now learned basic skating."

Wonderful! Now, that is the kind of wisdom and approach that I want in all of you, my dear grandchildren. Never be let down. You know, great leaders are forged from determination and the ability to bounce back from failure and keep going. If you give up easily, you will not be able to go far in life or in your ventures. So, don't be afraid to take risks. If you win, that's something to celebrate, and if you lose, take notes and make a lesson for the future out of it. Whatever you do, you learn, and that, I believe, is the biggest victory of all.

Now, my dear grandchildren, one thing that I should mention is that while you all will be given individual special phrases to work on when you are eligible, it is also of significant use to learn from each other's phrases. Like, for now, you have all received a lesson from D3's special phrase, and that is how you can all progress to become some amazing human beings.

Damian, you must work on your special phrase not just until you are 18 but for the rest of your life. Trust me, these phrases that we receive may seem like just a tradition, but they have the power to change your life and develop your personality. You will never be a loser, Damian, if you hold this phrase close to your heart in every adventure of life.

That's what the holidays are all about. Traditions, love, family, and growth. My grandfather once told me that traditions are the glue of a family, and I now tell you that.

Now, when you become grandparents, my dear grandchildren, you can take these words forward to your grandchildren. That is why we get together for our huge party every year and for our monthly get-togethers — to maintain our traditions, to celebrate ourselves, and in some cases, to give refuge to a world-weary, traveling family member, just looking to be with loved ones again.

The family heads were your great-great-grandfather Jidel, and great-great-grandmother, Arlisha. Jidel was a proud and brilliant man who worked hard for his family. When he was incredibly young, he left the southern part of the country to move to the North with his parents, brothers and sisters, uncles, and aunts.

Word is, one of his older brothers killed a Class 2 and had to flee because of something you may not know about. There was actually a time when the Lower Classes could not even eat in the same restaurants as the Upper Classes without suffering unspeakable acts. So, you know, if they killed a member of the Upper Classes, they got worse than the beating, lynching, and burning they got for being at the wrong place at the wrong time.

I never heard anything that disputed that killing, so it was one of those things generally accepted but never discussed. When it was discussed, though, it was said that this Class 2 man came up to my great Uncle Eliadad and his wife, Marisha. It was then said that things got out of hand, and Uncle ended up having to kill this Wanto in order to save their lives.

My grandmother, and your great-great-grandmother, was a stately woman who always seemed to have the answers. Very colorful and always cheery. Her strength was her beauty. She always wore bright and decorative clothing, and she used to always say, "If you got it, flaunt it!" as she would twirl and let her long dress flow as she gracefully flaunted.

Heh, everybody loved her, and the townsfolk all respected her. She believed in helping everyone and did a lot of volunteering in the community. They were each one of 12 children when they met and fell in love.

You know, it is crazy, but none of either of their 11 siblings had any children, and they had 12 children together! Sort of like my sister who had a daughter at age 21. That daughter, in turn, had a daughter at 21, and that daughter had her first child at, you guessed it, 21!

Each one of the three also had a son, thus one son and one daughter. Coincidence or fate?

"That was just for your edification. It is never a bad thing to be aware of your history. In fact, I encourage it. Marisol, tell us your lineage going back 7 patriarchal generations".

"Oh, Grandfather, you always ask me stuff," she quickly responds.

"It is because you speak so eloquently, my darling."

"And you always say that, too," she comes back.

Everyone laughs.

"Okay, there was the carpenter, Moses who was the father of Lucious, a very successful carpenter, who was the father of a tremendously successful carpenter named Martin, who was the father of Jidel, a doctor (I think he was adopted), who was the father of Khiray, a brilliant doctor, who is the father of you Grandfather, who is the father of Damian II, who is the father of me."

"Very well done, young lady. It is important that we know where we come from in order to know where we are going, guys, remember that." Now, who can tell me what Jidel was famous for?" How about you, Kaleb?"

"Grandfather, everyone knows that great-great-grandfather Jidel was one of the most well-known heart surgeons that ever lived. They have a procedure named after him." "That's exactly right, my dear. The 'Jidel Maze' from his amazing innovations in using scar tissue to block the electrical signals causing stroke and heart attack.

"You guys know why I remind you of that, right?"

"I don't quite understand," insists Marisol.

"Well, when one considers his origins and the struggles he endured, it is absolutely amazing and wonderful how he stretched his limits and put aside the will of the streets and his circumstances to pursue his calling. Of course, not everyone knows their calling right away or ever. But when you hear the calling, answer!"

How will you know when you are being called Grandfather?

"Listen to your heart, Darling, listen to your heart. But do not let your heart be corruptible. When your heart is filled with purity, it will not fail you."

Damian watched them and noticed that there was a real closeness among them. They supported each other through thick and thin.

Well, where were we? Oh yeah, Grandmommy, in her time, when it was still allowed, went to worship every week. When the government banned congregating altogether, people did their worshipping in secrecy. The pandemic didn't help either. Even if folks were legally allowed to congregate, the pandemic had folks shut in. You guys can understand that. I know you want to go hang out like you used to, but those days are over, and things are done quite differently now. So, when my family stayed with my grandparents briefly, there was one of many hard and fast rules that kind of shaped us all, and that was, if you want to go to the movies later today, you have to go to worship.

Grandmommy believed that if you were unable to go to worship, you had to be sick. And, if you were sick, you certainly were unable to go to the movies.

We loved going to the movies and even bore going to worship to get to see the latest "show." But after a while, worship was not so bad. We actually began to look forward to it.

I had my first crush on Miss Wilma, who conducted most of our classes. She was the smartest lady I knew, at least about worshipping. Of course, nowadays, only men can teach. Progress?

Anyway, we went early on Sunday mornings and attended a worship class. Then once class was over, we attended the worship services, with adults and children in attendance.

"I was always fascinated with the choir, and I am sure that shaped my opinion of worshiping from that point forward. You know that whole spirituality thing, the belief that there is a higher power? I never got into the fire and brimstone talks the preachers would give us as there always seemed to be something missing or off, for me."

"Grandfather, what do you mean about that "fire and bromerock, uh — br —""

"It's Brimstone, Kaleb," Rahij corrects.

Grandfather snickered and added, "That is what is considered to await those that did not do good in their lives. For doing bad things, they ended up in an eternal fire that burned with the help of something produced by lightning and symbolized divine punishment. Of course, that is an olden belief that is not very commonly shared these days. But it still bodes a terrible fate, and nobody living can say from experience if it is true or not.

Do not get me wrong; I do believe in a Higher Power. But I do not believe everything I was taught by them and I know firmly that there should always be faith, the very substance of all you hope for, even if you cannot see. But that faith has to be well-founded.

I only later in life discovered that these pastors were fleecing or deceiving everybody. This may all sound strange to you guys since all worship attendance was banned over 20 years ago, before you all were born, even before the revolt. In fact, most say that banning faith-based gatherings and practices helped fuel the revolt. But that was the first in an extensive line of lessons in patience and discipline for me. In my mind, two of the most important attributes one can have.

"Are you writing this down?" he surprisingly asks. "Yes, Grandfather, I never want to miss your talks! Plus, you did say take notes earlier." "Oh, ok. Anyway..." (chuckling)

Reminiscing and looking up as he spoke, Damian adds, "I especially remember the scents and aromas that always let us know what season it was. The smell of the cinnamon potpourri filling the air from a huge pot boiling on the electric stove, always set at the lowest temperature to make sure it simmered all night long, and of course, the smell of freshly baked mayonnaise cake, one of *my* mother's many specialties. Now I know that may sound gross, but until you have tasted one of her famous mayonnaise cakes, you cannot say a word.

"You see," he leans closer, looks side to side and whispers, "the secret is using mayonnaise instead of cooking oil, but then only real bakers know 'bout dat dere'!

CHAPTER 2
SUGAR AND SPICE

Families are always a mix of sugar and spice. They are like that cabinet in the kitchen where you can find so many differently smelling and tasting spices and whatnot that add flavor to your dishes. That is the thing, though; the differences between family members are what add taste and flavor to family life – that is something to cherish, I tell ya.

Now, kids, like you all have your uncles and aunties, your grandfather here has some wonderful, unique memories of my uncles and aunties, too.

Oh, there was always the distinct odor coming from our uncle Art. He was the family's black sheep, you know, heavy drinker, radical thinker, unpredictable, try to be just like him!

Uncle Art had that scent that comes from constant drinking. It oozed out of his pores and was always on his breath. His muscle shirts reeked of booze even worse than his breath. He always kept his bottle of encouragement in his left back pocket. When it was gone, he and his faithful companion, Ayluf, would walk to the local store to get another three bottles. They would each drink one slowly but immediately, and the other went into his back pocket as a backup. Now, children, don't take this as any encouragement, though. Drinking is definitely not a good habit, and the way Uncle Art did it, I still don't know how that guy even functioned in his daily life!

Heh, I remember one particular time when Uncle Art had had his daily libation, shall we say, and he was feeling no pain at that point.

We were a handful of children! Twenty in total – including all of us, my brother and sisters and cousins and friends. Imagine the yard full of twenty children of all heights and ages! So, all twenty of us were out in front of the yard, playing like every day. Again, this was a time when children could play outside their homes without interruption from government restrictions. There were no fears of muggers, kidnappers, or just bad people to threaten our daily good times. And before Martial Law, no one had to fear being shot for "Noncompliance of the law."

It was considered completely safe for kids to be let out, unlike later when even adults would be scared to walk out into the streets, let alone their kids. Anyways, on this particular day, a Class 4 Citizen (we did not call them by Class in those days, but we did identify them by their apparent status) approached all of us children while we were playing in the yard.

This man appeared repelling, to say the least. He was fat, dirty, and stinky. From his appearance, we could tell that he was obviously poor, homeless, and drunk when he decided to come up and started bothering us, children.

We were just kids, lost in our own little games, minding our own business, when this giant man came up to us, and he yelled at us and said something about us having no business having this much fun. He even reached for Jippi, my cousin the same age as me, and motioned as though ready to pick him up. We were all looking up at him with mixed feelings – none of them good, obviously, but feelings of shock, anger, and disgust. But what happened next is amazing!

Well, in his mid-stride, while turning up his bottle, Uncle Art, seemingly coming out of nowhere, hit this Dreg guy and knocked him out cold. One punch! That was all it took to put that stinky bastard to the ground. The kids, all twenty of us, cheered for our Uncle Art for the heroic action that he had taken for us. Despite his drunkenness, he loved us dearly and knew how to protect us.

He then finished his hit and customarily replaced it in his back pocket. The amazing part that I remember about that event is that Uncle Art was left-handed and had switched his drink from his left hand to his right hand and cold-cocked that man with his FULL left. Even while all this action was taking place, he never spilled a drop!

Among the twenty of us, three of my playmates were his children. Lisa, Art II, and Billy. I always enjoyed it when they came around as we were awfully close. Uncle Art was a strong man despite his deteriorating health. We all knew he drank too much, and we knew it would also one day be the death of him, or so my momma said several times. But he knew the value of family and would protect his family at all costs.

Uncle Art was an example of someone so into his beliefs that he sometimes did what could be called terrible things in defense of those beliefs. Hitting that man may not have been a good thing, but it became the right thing for Uncle Art. So, my dear children, that is where your values and your firm stand for those values come in. That is what makes you a strong person.

He even fought in the war along with one of his brothers, Uncle Rashad. They served across the sea in a foreign war in a distant land. I never really understood why they fought but then, who really, ever does? Times were such that people died, and no one knew why someone so close to them had to die. Class 1 and 2 families did not have to send more than one son to war, but apparently, our Class was the exception. No regard was given to whether two sons from the same family were killed for a war that was not even theirs.

I will explain to you later how it is so important to pick your battles wisely and choose the right fights for yourselves. None of your efforts should be wasted or futile – if you must fight, fight for a cause that you believe in.

My uncles being in the war must have influenced my decision to choose military service as one of my careers. Funny, my three uncles that did not go to war each had their own unique influence on me.

Too young at the time for service, they undoubtedly would have made the same sacrifices. Talking of my uncles, there was Uncle Wadud, the lover. Do not dare tell *anybody* this, but he was my *favorite*. I guess that was because he was loved by everybody, and he loved quite a few. Heh, heh!

He was really a good-looking lad. One of his wives was the most beautiful woman I had ever seen at my young age, and I figured, if he was with her, he had some serious game, or a really big schlong, or both!

"Grandfather!" demurs Etha, Damian's third grandchild and twin to Elihu.

Chuckling, he says, "Either way, he was my first hero."

Hehe, there was this one dance he did that will always be associated with him in my mind. I think it was called the Horse, and like most of the dances of that era, everything was a simulation for sex and sexual prowess. From the name of the dance even, I suppose you kids can figure it was not a very decent one! But either way, we enjoyed watching him dance and entertain us.

I admired how he knew who he was and lived life his way, just like how I admired Uncle Art's commitment to his family. Despite a person's flaws, it is wonderful when we can be loved because of what we mean or represent to someone.

Take my Aunt Rosa. At a youthful age, I did work for her around the house and yard for extra money. She was always so kind to me and would even fix a lunch for me. At the time, I thought the work was a bit hard and grumbled under my breath. She always knew and would quickly say something that only kinda made sense. One time though, she had tasked me with vacuuming the entire house. I did not dare complain though my face gave me away. She simply said, if you dig ditches for a living or if you run a major company, be the best ditch digger or company boss you can. That one I got! I am just glad that I was able to appreciate her while I could and not just in one-dimensional memories years later. To me, Aunt Rosa meant strength, wisdom, and uprightness, which I think are essential qualities for a woman.

It all goes back to doing the right thing by one's family, like Uncle Art. The kind and caring hearts, the subtle lessons, the love of family, and striving to do what was right. Sound advice, indeed.

Long before it was commonly accepted that each is an individual in their own rights, yeah, that time existed, everyone tried to be like the "it guy." You know what I mean: tall, ruggedly handsome, athletic, wavy hair, and just oozing with what was perceived as charisma, and able to handle any situation. A born leader.

Now, while I do encourage leadership as necessary in the properly girded man or woman, you have to know where to draw the line and know when it is too much. This is one of your challenges in life, my children. Power is a drug worse than any other drug, and if one lets it get to their head, there is a high chance that they will lose themselves to this drug and do all kinds of wrong things to keep feeding on it.

Accept your responsibilities and your leadership wisely. Know your limitations. You come from a strong legacy and have inherent responsibilities to maintain that legacy. Understand?

My dear grandchildren, true leaders are not chosen but rather born. I have seen too often over the years where leaders were chosen, and it was more out of popularity than anything else. The problem was, they were *not* leaders. They were just someone with the best promises or the most popular one that got chosen. A leader sees what needs to be done and gets it done, following instincts and the abilities within themselves. That is what I honestly believe in. But what kind of leader one becomes is up to one's own priorities and mindset. Remember one thing: If you are ever in a position of strength, never exploit someone who looks up to you from a position of weakness.

The exploitation of rights is the worst thing one can do with their power. Unlike the corrupt leaders that we have all witnessed so frequently, sadly, a true leader is one who facilitates his fellows, his friends, family members, and the people for whom he is accountable. A leader is not someone who scares his people into worshipping him and who strips the people of their rights to benefit himself.

You know, my dear grandchildren, my experience in the military taught me quite a few things, and amongst them were true leadership and responsibility. If you learn to take responsibility and be accountable for your actions, you will find that life is much simpler and you have a purpose. I know that you, my kids, are too young to understand or even apply these concepts now at this age. Still, I hope that my words will stay with you, and you will remember these words if you are ever presented with such a situation where they apply.

Interestingly, though, my dear grandchildren, the concepts of leadership and responsibility do not apply to only adults or authoritative scenarios, but also to you, as children. For example, I know that among all of you children, there are two or three children who act as informal leaders.

"Who, Grandpa?" Elihu asked innocently.

"Well, I am not going to name anyone, but I can tell you this: Observe it next time when you play a game or otherwise get together that there are some of you who are born leaders. Some of you naturally have characteristics of leaders like when you may dominate, command, or set examples in the group."

The basic idea is that when you lead people, lead them towards a worthy cause. Do not lead them astray, even if it could benefit you in some way. That is a real and responsible leader who knows and understands the importance and consequences of his leadership. And what is more important than that is that you lead your team, friends, and followers towards unity when you are a leader. If a leader amongst you cannot keep your followers united, then there is no team to lead in the first place.

My dear grandchildren, just like I told you about the sugar and spices in my paternal and maternal family, i.e., my uncles, aunts, etc., everyone has a different mix in their family. You might have uncles that you like or dislike, or aunts that you may get along better with as compared to others, or even neighbors who irritate the heck out of you when you play outside. The strength lies in ensuring that this mix of sugar and spice is enjoyed for what it is.

I learned, especially from my time away from home in the military, that the beautiful blend of what a family is cannot always be found everywhere else in the world. Being around your family members is a blessing, just like being around you all makes an old man like me happy. I feel proud to see how my family has extended, and several new branches have grown out of me, quite literally.

So, that is the bittersweet cycle of life, my children. Today, you are young like I once used to be. You have all the time to play and be worry-free. Use this time to learn and experience new things. Don't be afraid to fall because only after a good fall can you get rid of your fears by picking yourself up and moving ahead.

Families and friends are the elements that add flavor to an otherwise dull life, so hold on to them, my dear grandchildren, and cherish their presence in your life. You will grow into adults, carry out your life's missions, and then retire one day and become a grandparent like me. Then, you would be telling your grandchildren how you used to live back in the days. That's a cycle that time gifts us with, and not everyone is fortunate enough to live through this cycle, so never take it for granted.

You may even fight amongst yourselves some days. Some days, you might feel hurt by one another's actions or words. Still, on those days, I want you all to remember that you are not just siblings and cousins, but you are bound together by the blood you share and that no conflict is bigger than your pure, beautiful hearts.

"Wow, grandpa… You're making us really emotional now…." A sweet little grandkid sighed with eyes twinkling with a layer of dampness.

Ha-ha, really? That is because you love each other so much that you do not want to think about how different you might grow up to be. But that's the thing. You will all grow up to be different from who you are today – that is what makes a family a true sugar and spice cabinet, doesn't it?

It is good to have emotions, but do not let yourself be driven by emotions in life. Let your emotions guide you but not control you. Think with your heart, but always, always, do with your mind.

"Grandfather, you told us about the uncles and Aunt Rosa, but what about your other aunts? Do you have any of their stories?"

Of course! I just did not hang out that often with the aunts because they were mostly occupied with family functions, but yes, I have heard quite a few stories about my aunts… But you know what, I know better stories about *your* aunts, children! Why don't we talk about them?

There was applause from the group of grandchildren, but then some argued that they already knew their aunts and that they would like to hear stories of my aunts instead.

Well, okay… There was this… Ah, yes, there is a story about my Aunt Grace. She was an amazing artist, a great chef, and a perfectionist, but the one thing she was not was that she was not ready to be the mother of three naughty children.

I remember that I was hanging out with my cousins, her children one day at their home. She had a daughter and two sons. The daughter was younger, but both the sons were about my age, born maybe a year apart.

When I went there, as usual, I saw her dusting the shelves and vacuuming the carpet. It was her habit to tell anyone entering the house not to come in unless you have rubbed all the dust off of your shoes. Now, there was the homely smell of fresh buns in the kitchen, and she had served us cookies on the dining table soon after we had arrived there.

When we were kids, we were very bouncy and active – we could not sit still for long, so instead of being a disciplined kid, I nudged my cousins, i.e., her two sons, to go play outside with me. They loved the idea, and we ran out with the cookies in our hands. I am sure that we must have dropped a lot of cookie crumbs on our way to the garden, and she must have quickly mopped the floors after us.

Anyways, we played ball outside for quite a while before the ball landed into a puddle of muddy water. My cousins were well-aware of their mother's nature, but I was not. So, I jumped into the puddle to pick the ball up, and my cousins suddenly ran indoors. I was not sure why they ran away in the middle of the game, and I figured that their mother might have called them in, so I followed.

Unfortunately, when I ran back into their home, I was not too careful. My shoes left clearly noticeable muddy footprints all across the lounge's floor. I immediately felt a heavy gaze on me as I saw Aunt Grace with the mop in her hand staring at me in disbelief. Behind her,

her two sons were giggling uncontrollably, pointing at me – Oh, that's why they ran in. They wanted to get me into trouble just for fun!

So, anyway, as I saw the anger on Aunt Grace's face, I immediately froze and said sorry. I realized that the floor was wet because she had mopped the lounge and was almost done when I had run in. *Uh oh!*

Oh noooo!…. I thought she would yell at me or maybe complain about me to my parents, but instead, here is what happened: She fell to the floor, stunned. Her face was flushed, and soon enough, her lips pouted, and she started crying. As if that was not weird enough for me, she laid back on the freshly mopped floor with her arms and legs spread as she cried. She was always so dramatic!

I was so astonished and confused about what was happening. In my head, I was thinking, "Geez, relax, auntie… just mop again, it's just some mud," but of course, I knew better than to say anything at the time. I looked at my cousins, who were not laughing anymore. Clearly, they were confused about their mother's reaction, too. I stood there with my muddy shoes as my aunt cried about her unclean floors. Imagine the awkwardness!

Her daughter came into the lounge from her room, and when she saw this, she gave me quite a beating. Of course, I was rescued only when Aunt Grace was done mourning and decided that her daughter had punished me enough. As it turned out, Aunt Grace and Piper were all in on it. They had fun at my expense.

That was a very awkward day, but the next day when we all gathered, we could not stop laughing about the series of events. I had apologized over and over to Aunt Grace, but my mother told me that no one likes someone ruining their efforts, and I understood that Aunt Grace was passionate about the way she kept her house looking top-notch, and we, er I, had ruined that, so of course, she was disheartened, or at least she pretended to be. A lesson learned.

"Ha-ha, that sounds funny, Grandfather. Tell us more!" Nubia chimed.

Hmm… Let's do that some other day, kids, because I have a hundred such anecdotes! But, for now, tell me something… what have you all learned about family values today?

"To protect one's own, to forgive, to care," Etha showed off her understanding.

Very impressive, Etha! That is quite a comprehension of today's stories! More importantly, though, we have learned that a family has all sorts of people brought together by love, and not even one of them should be made fun of or looked down on. Families understand each other and support each other's skills, passions, and uniqueness in a way that no one else can.

Now, when you will all grow up, get married, and have children of your own, you will become the uncles and aunts of each other's children, too. So, love and respect each other to set an example for your generations to follow.

The girls in the group giggled at the thought of being aunts themselves.

"I would be such a cool aunt!" Nubia said to Elihu. "I will play with your kids and be their favorite!"

"No, I will play with my kids and be their favorite!" Elihu argued, almost offended as she felt possessive for the kids she didn't have yet.

How about you both play with your kids and be their favorites?

Everyone laughed as the two girls hmphed.

CHAPTER 3
THE PROTAGONIST

So, are you all ready for the story now?

"Yes, grandfather!" The children said in unison like a chorus.

This story, my dear grandchildren, is about a brave and responsible man. He had made a good fortune in life by selling a series of bestselling books and movies, but he was a man of wise decisions and invested his royalties and his time shrewdly. Smart moves pay well, and within five years, he had amassed a 4-comma fortune.

He lived through times much different than yours. When he was a kid, it was safe for children to play on the streets. There was rarely ever a case of abduction or kidnapping, and the parents could rest assured that playing outside was good for their children.

But, as he grew, he saw times change. Eventually, it became less safe for kids to play in their gardens or cycle around their streets because the government started killing them. It initiated quietly like the calm before the storm, but cases of such inhumane attacks grew.

"Killing them?" A little girl in the circle of grandchildren around asked with her eyes widened and her mouth open. "Why, grandpa?" She asked innocently.

"To scare the people. To impose their authorities and powers in order to rule every aspect of the people's lives."

It was a monstrous time. People were dying for no reason. The application of Martial Law was not officiated at that time, and yet, the government was already working as if it had. They were shooting people indiscriminately regardless of their innocence, age, gender, or even class. Some people were being fired for no reason other than the class they belonged to. Then, some people were being pushed out of their homes, and their properties were being taken over by political gangs. It was all chaos and no system.

At first, everyone thought that the injustice was directed only at the Dregs of Class 4, but gradually, everyone became unsafe at the hands of the government. The unjust and cruel acts were being directed at everyone after a few months, and it was no longer a war against a certain class but against everyone who refused to give in to their unfair system. Nobody was immune anymore to the ills of the corrupt governments.

You would not believe it, kids, but people were being shot – without warning, without any questions asked – for things as little as jaywalking. Noncompliance with the law became widely known as something punishable by instant death, and there was no one that the so-called authorities were accountable to. They held no responsibility and showed no remorse for the lives they were destroying. Our hero's world had suddenly started to change drastically.

The free public parks with crowds of kids and families celebrating their leisure time every evening were soon emptied. People were afraid to step out of their homes because even a little mistake could get their entire family killed. Humanity was breathing coarsely at its deathbed.

Our hero lived through challenging times when the government was planning various laws devious in nature to exploit and harm innocent citizens. Albeit the storm hadn't come yet – there were only talks and discussions about what should be done, and the evil intentions behind these plans were apparent.

There were implementations of some of those plans by world leaders who abused their power to wantonly take from others what they could for themselves. The first stages of an evil framework began from reducing farm subsidies, then to depleting educational tools and eliminating social welfare programs. The fatcats of government were spending like crazy and raising taxes and prices on everything. Our hero could predict that the *system* was going to get tougher to deny and more evil in nature. A new plan of action was being put into place.

Things were getting worse. Even the most remarkable of doctoral candidates were concerned that the government would seize their theories and years of arduous work. Their painstaking efforts and dissertations were all at risk of being weaponized, but this was all soon to end. The haphazard times that our protagonist was living through were going to change. They had to.

Our hero saw what needed to be seen and refused to let things be. This story is about Damian, the man who recognized the threat in time and devised a counter-action plan. Over the course of his life, he worked towards minimizing the threat to life imposed by the Martial Law and became a true hero, a champion, to many a people. That is what this story is about, but before that, let's discuss why our hero was even able to become a hero in the first place.

Like our Uncle Art, kids, our hero was protective of his people and believed in doing anything to make things right by them. To his advantage, he was always excellent at physics and electronics as a kid and was naturally fascinated with science. That made his logical side of the brain sharper than most kids his age, and ultimately, this highly developed IQ level helped him later in his life's missions, too.

"Like you, Grandfather? You were always great at physics and electronics, too, right?" Nubia, one of the sweetest little girls in my circle of grandchildren, chimed.

I smiled and nodded, "Similar, similar…."

Damian, our hero, like most other science lovers, was curious by nature. He liked to study, observe, and analyze situations in different conditions, and the changing times that he had grown up in had only sparked his curiosity further. He was always taking several variables into consideration, thinking about all viable solutions at a given time. He was constantly observing all problems in a given situation, too, while keeping a record of any external or internal factor that could directly or indirectly affect a problem.

Many others were concerned and curious like him, but they did not plan on taking any massive actions yet. People felt alienated in their own hometowns. They felt like the very people who were supposed to protect them were now their enemies. Naturally, as people felt disconnected from the government, they tried to connect more with each other to sustain a feeling of unity and societal familiarity.

Because, as I mentioned earlier, we all need a family. Those who did not have any families found familial love and support in their circle of friends and social acquaintances around their neighborhoods. In short, people had realized that the government was no longer holding their hands and that they had to hold each other's hands to stay connected and together.

Several groups were forming to discuss what the world had come to and what one could do at times like those. Damian had also joined diverse groups of concerned global citizens. Some people had started forming online groups to discuss these matters and connect with people far and wide all over the world, but the government authorities in place had even started monitoring and censuring that. In fact, it got to the point where anyone who messaged someone to share information or to invite them for a peaceful protest, or even showed contempt for the authorities, they would soon find themselves either in prison or staring down the barrel of a gun as armed government personnel would break into their houses and arrest them for 'disloyalty' to the government.

These little groups became secretive. They would often gather in a neighbor's house to discuss what the latest incidents of government cruelty the people in the society had faced and what could be done. They knew Martial Law was put into place; they needed a way to meet. Over the course of a few months, they were able to successfully construct a tunnel system that connected the houses. Things had gotten so terribly bad that they had to resort to this. Whatever it takes sometimes!

Damian reflected on the words of so many folks. "But is there really a way out of this mess?" An elderly mister thought out loud at one of the meetings Damian had attended.

"There is one way!" Damian proposed as everyone turned their attention to him. He cleared his throat before proceeding, "The only way to have a real, meaningful change is to remove every single politician from the face of this earth!"

Of course, despite the seriousness in his tone, he was applauded with laughter and claps. Apparently, his proposed solution was a light joke, and he knew that even if it weren't, it would never really happen. But little did he know that he would stumble upon an idea that could change everything and make even the impossible… possible. He was a hero who hadn't yet discovered his own potential yet.

As time went by, people lived with the cruelty. Some gave in to their power to save lives, while some stood strong against them in the face of danger, guarding their rights the best way they could, ending in the ultimate sacrifice, in some cases. Damian was among these people, too, who stood for their rights, willing to die for what he believed in. He was well in his 40s when he joined the fight. His love for technology would gift him an idea over which he would base his plan: His plan to save the world.

Meanwhile, there were more and more changes growing in the world. We were headed towards what was officially called the New

Norm. More changes and restrictions were introduced into people's lives when a seemingly harmless virus that had started some months earlier had begun spreading rapidly across the globe. From one corner of the world to another, too many people were being diagnosed with it. So much so that the governments of the world officially declared it a global pandemic. Whether the threat of this virus was real or not was another debate, but there were no doubts that it was a carefully planned and prepared strategy to make people obey them. Freelance journalist Arnold Miller wrote extensively on it, pleading for a course of action that did not seem to do more harm than good. His evidence included video, letters, emails, and everything." "What happened to him, Grandfather?" He began working with our hero. Our hero recognized early that Mr. Miller had remarkable research skills and a nose for the truth. He knew he could use a man of his talents and that he had to protect him. And protect him he did. But more on Mr. Miller later.

As if things were not already disappointing, the government had apparently started propaganda using this virus as the basis. Our hero observed how all of a sudden, every death in the world was being attributed to this newly formed virus. It took only a minute's thinking to knock sense into oneself about the imposed global situation.

The pre-pandemic death statistics showed people dying from cancer, blood diseases, accidents, and old age quite commonly, of course. But, after the pandemic hit, suddenly, people were dying only from the virus and not from cancer, old age, or any other disease like before? It was an obviously fishy situation, and Damian smelled its stink from afar.

"Looks like this virus has cured cancer and all other ailments!" He joked in another one of his group discussions.

Not only our hero but several other people were now beginning to realize that the virus, real or not, was being used by the governing authorities to control our lives more than they ever did. Martial Law was over, and the democratic rule had begun, but it was no different than Martial Law. Instead of the guns and armed men killing people, it was a virus that eased into a sea of people to manipulate their minds by using their fear of death to make them obey their authorities.

The media was in on it, too. In fact, the entire propaganda was run through the media to brainwash innocent people. Television, radio, newspapers, newsletters, social media, everything was used. A sudden wave of fear for life had been injected into the masses through the continuous manipulation of information. While professional journalism and news reporting call for the reporters to be very calm and composed and disseminate information in a tone that does not cause chaos, the news in the time of the pandemic was being told in high-pitched, scared voices with a sense of urgency to call for people's attention and make them scared. They wanted this. They wanted the chaos because it would confuse people, distract them from the injustice of the governments, and direct them to ask for help from their authorities.

Yet, even at a time like this when people were dying left and right, our so-called leaders did not back away from taking selfish advantage out of the pandemic. Leaders of the nations became opportunistic and took advantage of the very people they swore to protect.

"Grandfather, where were you at this time? Did you see the pandemic?" A curious grandchild asked in the midst of the story.

"I was there, living among the many who stood against the governments. Yes, of course, I lived through the pandemic! It was horrific to see how everything was changing. Hell, even a 'new normal' was introduced!"

Our hero saw this fear progress into an attempt to manipulate and gain control over people. He saw the governments corner people through the fear of this pandemic and then impose their power over them. This is exactly what Damian hated. An extension of the control of evil men over innocent ones. How can any world leader just take, take, and take, and give nothing in return?

Will our hero just sit and watch? Or does he have a plan brewing in his remarkable mind?

"Ohh, I can already tell he is going to have an amazing plan! Otherwise, he wouldn't be the hero!" The smartest boy in the circle replied enthusiastically.

You're right. He would not be a hero otherwise. After all, it was all thanks to just one plan that he was able to achieve his goals. One idea, my dear grandchildren… Just one idea is enough to change the world. Just one smart idea can make you into a hero, too.

CHAPTER 4
TIMEBOUND

I cannot stress enough how times changed drastically, kids, during those times. I was just wondering whether it was the pandemic or the digitalization of life in general, or a combination that changed everyone's lifestyles. I remember that I used to enjoy outdoor sports, and for a long time after I grew up even, I saw your parents enjoy outdoor sports. But now I see that there is much less physical activity. So I know times had to be bad for our hero.

"What were the sports back in your days, Grandfather?"

Oh, we had a lot of them. We used to play rugby, basketball, and football were special favorites among my friends. There were days when we would even go to the beach and enjoy the sunlight caressing our bodies until we could appreciate the beauty of its presence. Waterskiing, swimming, all great pastimes. Nature was still enjoyable before the Martial Law was implemented. Sigh... they messed things up too much.

You know, kids, there were even teams competing on national levels to go play sports in other countries. They were paid to play sports, mainly football or soccer, depending on where one is from. There were competitions and matches on massive levels. Winning one of these was a huge honor, a respectable accomplishment for a player and his team, and even the country that they were representing. Literally, thousands would be in attendance. And the world seemed to come to a standstill while the world's fans enjoyed this entertainment.

It's funny how things, events, and fads continue to recycle. The sports fans of the world have enjoyed watching their gladiators compete for thousands of years.

The events adapted to changing times, equipment, rules, etc. But at the end of the day, it still amounted to a competition to death.

"You mean they were killing each other, Grandfather?" Marisol asks.

"Well, when they began enjoying these events, it was a battle to the death. As time progressed, the killings were replaced with activities more inclined to show athletic ability and prowess. Sports developed and evolved, and when it was all said and done, it is still enjoying gladiators.

But when the Martial Law was imposed and then when the virus-induced pandemic hit us, it seemed as if the world lost its colors and turned into a dull gray. It's like they took the melody from our lives.

Honestly, the pandemic did not do this. It only worsened it. People had already become too involved in their digital devices to leave the house, and the kids followed in the same patterns. Instead of playing outdoors, kids started staying indoors playing video games, and when the pandemic was declared, people were further encouraged to stay indoors. What a joke! Since when is staying indoors a healthy lifestyle?

You know, my dear children, I used to love going bowling and playing golf, but now such activities are restricted. Your grandfather was quite a golfer. Not like the professionals, of course, but like poker, you fake it till you make it. I could always manage at least two award-winning shots each round, so imagine where I could have gotten to if golf didn't die out.

"Golf? I have it on my gaming console. You want to play it, grandfather?"

That is incredibly sweet, my grandchild, but no. Golf is not just about playing with a stick and a ball. It is about so much more than that. It is about the thrill of executing the perfect shot. It is about enjoying the environment as we played in the greenest parks of our time. I think it will be a long time before people start indulging in those outdoor activities again.

Now, more board games and electronic entertainment sources have become common. In fact, you would be surprised to know that I went to school with the guy who invented all those home games that are all the rage now. The industry paid him well, and it wouldn't be a surprise if one of you came up with a unique idea that sells well in this 3-comma industry.

The truth is that this plague, this pandemic, ruined everything. Especially with poverty being used as the reason to constantly reclassify people into lower classes due to worsening economic conditions created by the government. It was up to the few of us to carry the torch and lead our people towards a stronger future. Not one where we would have to live in fear like we were.

The government had crossed boundaries and had entered our homes through strategies – not physically, but in their authoritative forms. From confining our breaths behind masks and distancing us socially and physically, the governments had changed the norms of regular life. The surveillance techniques they used took invasion to a whole new level. The 'New Norm,' they called it. However, the New Norm was not so new, but a rather well-planned strategy that was in the making for years before it was finally unleashed. From what our hero found through extensive studies and research on the matter, the new normal was all part of the New Norm that was established centuries ago.

So, you see, the powerful authorities had planned centuries ahead of their time to maintain their control over the people.

As I saw it, the New Norm was just the ultimate version of attempts to control people. I don't know what it is about power, my kids, but these people seemed drunk off of it. As if one's own life is not interesting enough, these powerful people worked in mysterious ways to make everyone else their puppets.

Schools had shut down, businesses were failing miserably at survival, let alone profitability, and the world was coming to a New Norm that no one enjoyed other than those who were imposing it. The rich got richer, and the poor got poorer. That was life as we knew it, or as our hero knew it back in the day.

My dear grandchildren, you cannot know the importance of freedom of living until it is taken away. Each home had become a prison in itself in those days. We were all confined within our own walls, and this confinement had resulted in people developing mental health disorders, too.

Imagine if you had to stay in your bedroom for a full year! Wouldn't you become depressed and lonely, too?

"I would! I get tired of video games so soon, Grandfather!" Nubia volunteered her response to support my argument.

"Grandfather," one of the twin girls said questioningly, "Was the New Norm a part of Martial Law?"

"No, dear. It took up where Martial Law left off. But they are basically one and the same. Only timing separated the two."

The New Norm was designed with specific intents: intents that had no interest of the common man in mind. Intents that were there to strip away the remaining rights of people, leaving them defenseless against the government's weapons. They had entangled the people in this fear of dying from the virus so much that all the people could care about was living according to the precautionary measures so that they would not catch the virus. Little did they know, it was all a front, a façade to hide what was actually going on behind the scenes.

As if this was not enough, it was soon after the imposition of this New Norm that the Martial Law was declared again. It had not even been off for much time anyway – and it was now declared again. The government then put into place what I believed to be a brilliant but evil move; they changed the voting laws. They put restrictions on who could vote against them. The majority of Class 4 was included in this latest move. With every passing month, the government's grasp on the necks of common people was tightening, further suffocating them into succumbing to the forced lifestyle.

My children, it was a strange time. In our hero's long, long life, he had seen no times stranger than then. But your hero was working to turn things around, and he knew the people of the world were definitely not okay with being pushed around like that.

There was a time when the world was resplendent. There used to be children playing in the streets. The crossroads used to be busy with the traffic of people coming and going. You know, my children, the world was much greener then than it is now. "Is that what that word resplinter, er respl.." "Yes, dear. Resplendent means greener, dazzling, alive!

Your parents have always been outgoing and lively people. They would gather around on holidays and celebrate each other's presence. The freedom to celebrate our holidays – even that was taken away by the New Norm. Remember the family gathering I mentioned in the Winter Tales section of the story? That was all at risk – forbidden by the government. One year we even had to cancel our event. Imagine being grounded by the government in such a way that you cannot meet your own family members… not even on Holiday!

Initially, the New Norm was just introduced as a normal way of life rather than a law. There were recommendations to follow it, but not penalties to not follow it.

"It is for your own safety," the leaders said as if they cared about us. An extensive list of precautions against the virus was regulated from the first world countries to the third world countries.

"What is a first-world country, grandfather?" One of my curious grandchildren asked.

"It is a developed country. Superpowers. Like America. And, before your curiosity sparks again, let me tell you that third-world countries are underdeveloped or poorer countries."

All of a sudden, life became abnormal. Many people conformed to the regulations to safeguard themselves and their loved ones. Eventually, the *recommendations* turned into *impositions*. The suggestions to keep oneself safe from the virus were now rules to be followed. Mandatory rules to continue living in the society under the influence of powerful authorities looking for more ways to control our lives. Rules that limited how we lived."

"That sounds like a pretty mean group of guys, Grandfather."

"Yes indeed, yes indeed."

It was soon after the New Norm had established that the world seemed to have decluttered. We were all there – though many of us were dying every day, sometimes from the virus, sometimes from other ailments, but apparently only from the virus as that is what the media kept broadcasting – yet, we were all kept hidden in our houses.

When one would leave the house during that damned era, one would see empty streets that appeared to be hospital corridors with only a few people moving around with face masks, safety gloves, and protective clothing.

"Sounds like an apocalypse," the other of my twin girls stated as her eyes were wide with amusement.

"Sure. It was like living through an apocalypse," I answered, affirming her fear for how the world was so different back then.

You would be surprised to know, kids, that the 'welcome' signs from all shops had been replaced with a list of safety precautions to take before entering there.

1. No entry without a mask.
2. Get your temperature scanned.
3. Stay at home if you have symptoms.
4. Stay six feet away from other people.
5. Get vaccinated

Instead of a salesperson greeting you as you entered the shop, there would be a person in overall protective clothing checking your temperature with a gun-shaped scanner. Hah! What a way to live, to live with such fear!

Honestly, kids, the first time I saw one of these scanners being pointed at my forehead as I went to do some groceries, I felt like a gun was pointed at my head! And wasn't it? Wasn't it really a metaphor for guns pointed at our heads?

Some people were still rebellious, though. They were stubborn and refused to even accept the existence or threat of a virus. They would not wear the masks or would try to hold protests to be allowed to live their life freely again. After all, the taste of freedom was too good to forget.

But the government was not going to let that happen. It was not going to let a few rebellious people put any clever ideas in the others' heads. So, they were kept silent and shut away in any way they could. Eventually, there were heavy fines and penalties imposed for not following the safety precautions. Governments had officially announced through media platforms that there were only a given number of reasons that one was allowed to leave their own house:

1. To buy groceries or medicines.
2. To exercise in the open air.
3. To go to work (only those sectors that were allowed to operate regularly like the fuel and medical industries).

"What if someone died, Grandfather? Or, what if a friend was sick? Could you leave your house to visit them?" A question arose among the group of grandchildren.

"Only in unusual circumstances, dear. You could not visit someone even if they were dying of the virus, but you could go to help someone out as long as you took all the precautions and followed all the rules created for it."

Even the funerals were limited to a given number of people so that no crowd would gather. Basically, my dear children, all activities that involved people getting together were forbidden. We, as a people, were dictated to live without freedom.

"Was the virus really that dangerous, Grandfather?"

"No, honey. Our hero didn't think so. He was among those who believed that the virus was a cover for the higher level of radiation being introduced. He had researched that each time the government introduced higher levels of radiation when they increased traffic capacity and network efficiency, there was a pandemic where folks were dying. Their signs were always the same, and they all had flu-like symptoms.

Our hero was tired of living through such times with all its deceit and impositions. The world had to change. And, not only our hero, but most people saw the ridiculousness of those times. A lot of things did not add up. How, all of a sudden, a virus that had never been known before had emerged and ruined so many lives was beyond our hero's comprehension. He and many other people believed that the virus was produced and released for a defined purpose – it had not just been born out of the blue. In fact, our hero also believed that it was being used as a bioweapon of some sort on a lower level.

"What does that mean, Grandfather?"

Um… It means that instead of waging a full-blown war with guns, tanks, and all that, a biological weapon or something that affects a person through their physical anatomy. Poison gasses and anything that could deliver particles to the air one breathes was the more often used method. This was being used to kill people and perform a sort of cleansing of the populations.

"But how would that benefit them?"

Good question! They had a goal, dear grandchild. They had specific goals for everything in their plan, and similarly, they had specific population goals, too. The world was very populated, and obviously, more people meant tougher management. So, in order to be able to keep control of every individual, they aimed to reduce the population of the world to be able to maintain their control over them.

Since the Martial Law had been imposed and people were being compromised of their rights too easily, it was time to do something. To stand up and fight.

It was only after two years of oppression that people stood up in a united front. Factions cropped up all over, and before long, a global civil war broke out.

Yes, my children, so much had changed in just a short period of time. But our hero was not just going to sit back and watch this unfold. This story is about a man with a vision. A story about a man with conviction. Our hero, Damian, was a man of remarkable talents, and I want to tell you about the life he lived – a life of bravery, intelligence, and action.

Time and chance change each one of us and the world altogether.

While preparing for our hero's 20th high school reunion, he thought back to how high school life used to be and how all his friends had now grown, developed, and changed over the years.

Our hero had a vast knowledge of technology, thanks to his love for science. At this reunion, he was engaged in a deep conversation with a few of his fellow alumni.

They were all sitting in a group when Solomon insisted, "The government is so pathetic."

He was a black-haired friend of his and had a cigarette clutched between his two fingers. Our hero was a good talker and always liked being involved in discussions that interested him. This discussion about the government's injustice was one of his favorite topics, anyway.

"They wait so long to introduce innovative technology to the public as a matter of practice," Solomon proposed. "They have literally forced the world to use and rely on 5-nanometer chips forever. I mean, the technology already exists for smaller chips and more transistors per chip. In fact, 3-nanometer chips are already leaked, but they will not release those until they deem it is the right time. Ugh!"

Smaller chips were better; our hero agreed with his friend and had set forth an argument. He explained the reasons to support his claim, too. One, that smaller chips can be delivered with more ease, and two, those smaller chips were capable of being developed for more creative purposes.

"Very interesting, indeed," another group member agreed.

However, what Solomon had said was stuck in Damian's mind for a long while, well after the discussion was over. Those words about nanometer chips were ringing in his ears when he excused himself from the group and walked away towards other alumni groups.

"Truly, modern chips are capable of so much. I think their true potential hasn't even been explored yet."

Coincidentally, this other group was also having a conversation about the capability of modern chips and how they are underutilized. He listened to Jimi's ending statement in the conversation as he walked towards him.

"Yeah, I have done extensive study on the abilities of a chip and its relation to its transistors, and I can assure you that we can now create such transistors that act like time-released mechanisms," Jimi stated impressively. "We can even time the release based on command or situation."

Jimi was Damian's old friend, and I was delighted to see him. When the conversation progressed, and as Damian was asked for his opinion on the matter of governmental control, he stated, "Uh… I have a rather unrealistic solution, but a solution, indeed. I believe the only way to fix the anarchical state in existence is to rid the Congress of those bad seeds altogether and start replacing them or altering them one by one."

"You mean, wipe out the government altogether?"

The group had a nice laugh and cheered for his solution, supportive of the idea. Yet, Damian was a different person. He decided to do something else. Something very different.

He had decided that he would set out to change the mindsets of the people who sat in the office. He wanted to reform as many of them as possible and force the rest to resign. As unrealistic as it seemed, our hero was certain that this decision had potential, and he knew that he had to think about this seriously.

This very thought became the basis of how our hero realized his life's mission and the solution to the whole problem of the authorities. This discussion at the high school reunion stayed in his mind for long enough to cook up an idea that could cause massive changes.

CHAPTER 5
MEN WITH A PLAN

How dare I take on such a responsibility? Our hero thought and was soon answered by his own conscience: *How dare I not take on this responsibility?*

Our hero had already decided his plan of action. He had even employed some of the best men and women he knew to get started on its execution. He would employ Arnold Miller to start a campaign. Arnold would use his eloquent and persuasive words to write the sentiment of the people, and Damian would transmit the words in his newsletter. The newsletter that would reach millions around the world. Damian would use Arnold's words and follow it up with a meeting to inform the leaders of the struggle to gain as much support as possible. Damian lived in a massive three-story home whose backyard eventually became the meeting ground for many dedicated souls, and now, all the men and women who our hero had invited to discuss his plan.

They could only be impressed by Damian's intelligent solution, at the planned, large gathering, with scores of people from all the Classes where he would unveil the plan. From what they knew, that meeting would prove to be the most critical meeting to date on the struggles they all faced.

The day before the big *Pow-Wow!,* the five people sat in the conference room of our hero's house with overly concerned looks on their faces. This was where they met to discuss the most important and secret matters of their agendas, and the plan they were discussing now was going to change the world. *For the better,* they hoped. It was a very risky plan, and their concern was justified, but our hero was confident that it would work. If it malfunctioned even slightly, everything that could go wrong would go wrong with the world. *As if there isn't enough wrong going on already,* Damian thought.

Before the struggling began, they were a group of eight, but now, these five men had to carry the torch to continue the work they had started.

"Struggle? You mean standing up against the oppression Grandfather," Nubia asked, confused.

"All in good time, my dear. But yes, the struggle against oppression."

So, where were we?

Ah, our hero was seated with his four men in the conference room. Our hero's conference room had a huge table in the room, seemingly out of place. It was oversized in proportion to the rest of the room's furniture and formation, but that only stressed its purpose. My kids, that conference table was not an ordinary one. It was ten feet by eight feet and had a total of fourteen seats – six on each side and two on the ends.

Imagine with me, if you will, and you would feel like you are in that conference room, my beloved grandchildren.

"Yes, Grandfather! I'm imagining it!" One of my little boys said with his eyes closed.

The conference table had a beautiful design carved along its edges. It was made of the finest Muninga Cherrywood, a rich wood imported from the Light Continent where the best of all cherry woods were grown. The table was breathtakingly beautiful, with its gloss enough to illuminate the entire room.

"Was our hero very rich, Grandfather?"

"Uh… not *very*, but yes, I guess you can say he had better resources than many of that time."

In the center of the rectangular-shaped table, there was an opening that had a wading pool of tropical fish on the floor. There was a purple tang and a few lined surgeonfish that added colors to the room. Our hero liked that effect. He believed that the fish and the water produced a calming effect in the room, which was essential to prevent emotionally charged arguments when making important decisions. That table, my dears, was the center of critical decision-makers where often life and death scenarios were resolved.

You can presume all five of those people as your heroes, or at least your side-heroes because our hero alone could not have saved the world as effectively as he did. Remember, children, even heroes need support. We are all social creatures, and we are naturally inclined towards other human beings for different forms of support, motivation, relief, and friendship. We seek approval and inspiration in each other's actions and words. Yes, even the heroes need that. We have talked about friendship, haven't we?

"Just like we are there for each other, Grandfather?"

"Yes, my darling, just like all of you love each other despite all the petty fights you get into."

Just like a brother stands for a sister and vice versa, our five heroes planned on standing up for society. For humanity, for justice to prevail, and for evil to accept defeat.

I see you all sitting there in this large group around me, my dear grandchildren, and I feel so warm in my heart. This is how I always want you all to be. Be there for each other. Protect each other's interests. And, when one of you starts going astray, all the rest of you must help them find a way back home. That is what friends do for each other.

"But we are cousins, grandfather, not friends," A little girl with a pout pointed out innocently.

Cousins are a two-in-one package, dears! They are your family members and your friends – all in one! And that is what makes them even more special. They are your siblings, too, and the bond of friendship that can emerge out of this relationship is stronger than most.

So, where were we?

"The huge rectangular table, Grandfather! With the life and death situations!" The twin girls chimed in together.

Ah, yes! The table. It appeared to be a unique, royal one. There were regally styled chairs around it. I already mentioned it had fourteen seats, right?

Each of those chairs had a high back to support the heroes' strong posture. They were all draped in luxurious, full-grain leather with multiple dimples that gave it a very ravishing appeal.

"Does any one of you know what full-grain leather is?"

The group of grandchildren looked at each other to see if anyone knew the answer and then hummed a soft chorus of 'No's as they nodded to match their responses.

"It is like the one I have in my room's one-seater sofa. You have all seen that one."

So, the full-grain leather has been a proven material for its amazing durability, and that is why it was on those chairs around the conference table. As one would enter the magnificent room, the structuring of this royal furniture would present a beautiful view. One that would take one's breath away as one would gaze around the room to appreciate its look helplessly.

Three of the fourteen chairs were now leaned onto the table with their high backs resting against this magnificently crafted piece of furniture. The display of this served as a constant reminder of the price of freedom. It portrayed the heavy price of the sacrifices made for the struggle of their cause. The cause to free humanity from the unjust control of the puppet masters.

Our five heroes ensured that their morale was always high. A testimony of their dedication to their goals was the scores of photos, plaques, and certificates that hung on the wall to serve as a reminder of what struggle means. Some of these photos showed portraits of fallen heroes. These portraits symbolized that our heroes were willing to sacrifice even their own lives to facilitate the achievement of their goals to save the people and save the world. That is the patriotic spirit one must have.

"What do *fallen heroes* mean, Grandfather?" One of the youngest in the circle asked.

"Heroes who died fighting for us. For our country and its way of life."

There were also photos of friends, family, and happier memories of the days and years that had passed. Tributes to philanthropy and community service were also hung on those walls with pride. After all, our heroes, all eight of them, were proud of their accomplishments and were planning to accomplish more.

Damian, the hero, followed in his grandmother's footsteps. He was a perfectionist, especially when it came to him being the consummate host of these meetings. He ensured that every attendee of the meeting was well addressed in terms of hospitality. He would have tea ready for them all when they would arrive, and they would sip from their cups as they talked around the huge rectangular table. There were always some snacks or a meal lined up after the meeting would end so that none of the attendees had an empty stomach when they left. And tea, of course, was a great beverage to host people over, especially for important discussions such as the one our hero was having.

My dear grandchildren, at this point, I'd like to run a little disclaimer for all of you. When I tell you these stories or these details of our hero's behavior and attributes, it is not to convince you to be a certain way or not to be a certain way. I simply like to provide enough information for you, beautiful young minds, to make a sound decision yourselves. You can always find inspiration in these details and decide what you should or should not incorporate into your own lives. Remember, my children, every story comes with a moral, but all the details that make up a story and its characters are no less significant either.

For a long time, the concepts of right and wrong have been blurry. What we know today as wrong and right are merely dictated terms of what fit specific criteria by those who ruled before us. These criteria were formulated by previous leaders, by different traditions, and shaped by several events. There are some fundamental grounds to decide the alignment of any action being right or wrong, like anything that harms people is definitely wrong, but every situation has its own merits and demerits that determine the justice of any action.

What I like for you, my kids, is to have enough knowledge to decide correctly about your actions. The dictated criteria of right and wrong frustrate people. The worldwide revolt that I will tell you about soon was standing against that, in part. Now, when you have the right morals, making a sound decision is an easier task. That's where I come in, in your lives, to set your morals right and to give you the knowledge you need to live your lives.

As you will all grow up into adults, you will all become the heroes of your own stories. At that stage of your life, my dear grandchildren, you will face a lot of conflict with yourself, and all your wisdom will be tested then. Some decisions you may make might turn out to offend those around you but will reap desired results, while some of your decisions might be to please the people you love, but those decisions might fail your goals. Either way, life is tricky, and one must be wise to get through it successfully. It is like learning how to swim – if you're not a skilled swimmer, you might find it difficult to swim against a strong current in order to reach your destination.

Anyways, back to the meeting, guys! Our hero, Damian, and his crew were meeting to finalize the details of their plan. The first milestone they had decided on was holding a big meeting to disseminate their idea. That would clarify where the people of the society stood on the matter and how much support they could have to carry out their plan effectively. The five men at the table discussed the big meeting to be held: The Meeting of the Classes, they named it. The big *Pow-Wow!*

"Grandfather, who were these other heroes, and why had our hero chosen them?" Nubia asked.

Very good question. Let's introduce the other heroes now. There was JW, the right-hand man to the most powerful man in Class 2. You kiddos remember what I have explained to you about the different class systems, right? Nods in assent. JW was a very tall man with a long flowing beard. He loved to dress and could rarely be seen not wearing a suit and tie. He was teased because he was considered a man 'not afraid of colors.' He wore purples and golds and reds with no shame at all. He actually looked good in his suits, but it was a mistake to tell him. That's what he wanted to hear! He was a man of many talents, but his boss deemed his ability to foretell most valuable. His superpower foretold what was about to happen, and he was always accurate in his skill. For instance, he could tell you how a person would react in a certain situation or how a situation would likely unfold.

As you may predict from this information, JW had most notably foretold the worldwide pandemic and the world's leader's reactions to 'coping with it.' It was a vision that helped spark our hero's 'extracurricular activities.' His accuracy about the pandemic and other events provided JW with much credibility, particularly with the most influential of Classes 2 and even of 1, but only one person knew the source of JW's power, which was Damian, our hero. In fact, Damian had made JW the second in authority after himself in the group.

"Did all of them have superpowers, grandfather?"

Yes, but they were not the superpowers that you are thinking of. They could not make themselves invisible or climb up walls or throw spider webs! They had different kinds of superpowers like JW could see the near future, in a way.

Then, there was our hero's younger brother, Arctay. He was a big man as well and a cool character unlike any other. He enjoyed looking good and was the type to wear his tailored suits with white shirts but no ties. Even at the most formal of events, Arctay wore no tie. He was smart, funny, charismatic, and totally on top of the finances. Any related subject would come up, and Arctay would already be looking at calculations, algorithms, and pie charts flashing before his eyes. His mind worked like a calculator – fast and logical.

Even though Arctay was our hero's brother, he had no problem with JW being the second on the team. He was relaxed and content with his life, never failing to contribute his best efforts to achieve goals rather than achieve a certain position in the group. He believed that one should embrace their best-suited areas of expertise rather than try to be all over the place, and he lived according to this belief as he held on to what he excelled at; finances.

That is a very important lesson for you all, too, my dear grandchildren. These days, people are so passionate about winning that they forget to enjoy the process. They are so obsessed with reaching a certain position in life that they would cheat, lie, betray, or do whatever they think should be done to achieve that position. But, let me tell you, there is no satisfaction in being in a position where you cannot enjoy your full potential. Like Arctay, you should focus on giving your best efforts and reaching your full potential in any given task instead of worrying about the race that everyone is so caught up in these days.

Then, there was Damian's first and oldest cousin, Wilgred. Wilgred was a bit shorter than the first two but a man of great stature, nonetheless. His presence always made him seem 10 feet tall. When he entered a room, and folks heard him speak, all eyes would magnetically turn to him. Never a man who spoke to hear himself speak. No, he was knowledgeable on a variety of subjects, and when he spoke, it was advised to listen. He had studied law and was a brilliant prosecutor of Class 1 and 2 offenders before joining this group, inspired by his role model and cousin. He even taught law online. He was a fair man who had the skills to win more cases, but he saw the faults in the system as the big fish kept getting away, and he gladly walked away from that life.

"Who were the big fish, grandfather?"

The big fish means the politicians or other influential figures. They had their grasp on every authority and organization. They could always tilt the things in their favor to get out of trouble. Hell, they could even get away with murder.

"When the system is flawed, nothing you do will ever be good enough," he said as he expressed his wish to work with Damian towards a better world – a fairer world where justice halted those who tried to assert their power over lower classes.

As time progressed, they succeeded in rendering that 'power' futile against the masses of these lower classes, thanks in part to the efforts of Damian and his crew. Wilgred was loyal to these morals and values, and that was his forte and strength. That was his superpower.

One of the smartest guys in the group and a childhood friend of Damian was Aelio. Aelio was a smaller-framed man who wore huge glasses. Now Aelio was a looker and a charmer. He was always arrayed in the latest fashions that had him matching from his head down to his shoes. His shoes had to match his hat, which had to match his belt, which had to match….you guys get it. While he was devoted to his wife and 10 children, he would get offers every day from strangers, ladies he met a year ago, friends of his wife, all kinds of women were always coming up to him. Of course, it didn't hurt when you consider he had lots and lots of money. But, present any situation to him, and he would perceive it as a challenge or a puzzle to solve.

"Once all the pieces are visible, the solution becomes clear, no matter how damaging that solution could prove to be," He would say.

"Grandfather," Khandi interrupted. "What do you mean by that? Can you give an example, please?"

"Well, there was a certain time when a judge himself was accused of a crime. Arctay believed him to be innocent, and he could not let an innocent get punished, so he dug into the case himself. The judge was actually his brother, too. As it turned out, the judge was actually being blackmailed."

"Ooh," the whole gang of kids gasped in shock.

"Who was the bad guy, Grandfather?" Khandi asked out of curiosity.

"The mayor, but let's not go too deep into that."

The people loved the mayor for what he did for the city, but Arctay needed to choose between his brother and the city's mayor. When he found several more misdeeds conducted by the mayor, he worked around a way to save both of them actually. Even though he could have exposed the mayor, it meant exposing somebody who seemed to do good but was not really worth falsely convicting someone innocent. Do you know what I mean? He saved both of them, but it did cost.

"Yes, Grandfather!" Elihu's voice echoed as she answered confidently.

"Great, I'm so proud of you, guys!"

Okay, where were we? Ah, yes! Aelio.

Aelio was one of those people who always got the job done. He was reliable and got work done by any means necessary.

"So, Grandfather," Damian III intruded with flair and attitude, "was he like nonviolent-any-means-necessary, or *ANY* means necessary?"

"He was a little of both, actually."

Aelio used whatever resources he deemed fit to get the job done – that was his only goal. He was quick to assess situations and to act cleverly upon them. His mind worked very fast. Within seconds, he would observe, analyze, and comprehend a situation and act quickly according to it.

Aelio had met our hero in first grade, where they competed for the coveted RR Steele Award for Most Outstanding 6th Grade Boy. Our hero won the first position, and Aelio came in second, and ever since, he developed a true respect for Damian, and they got closer as friends.

Do you see why he, Aelio, is one of our heroes? He had the characteristics of a true hero, i.e., he did not become envious when Damian won the first prize even though they were just kids at the time of the competition. Despite Aelio's competitive nature and his obsession with achieving the goal, he started to respect the person who won, i.e., Damian. I want you to learn these little characteristics, my kids, because positive characteristics like these are what make people into heroes.

Damian was wise to choose his words and was the voice of reasoning in the group. With natural qualities, the group followed him as their leader. He embodied every attribute of his cohorts and brought power, money, charm, shrewdness, good looks, and a mesmerizing voice to the table. His visions allowed them all to continue their work for the struggle, and those visions were encouraged by JW.

Being a smooth talker, he took on lobbying duties for his union. He even appeared before Congress to persuade them on certain issues. His ideology was to help people see the bigger picture so that he could compel them by reasoning.

He was a man with a plan, and that plan was simple in its nature. Wilgred, as per his best skills, had checked and rechecked the details to find any loopholes, and everything was set. Their plan was foolproof. Now, there was the first step to take towards its execution: The Meeting of the Classes.

CHAPTER 6
THE MEETING

It was finally time for the meeting of the Classes. The big meeting that was so meticulously prepared for by our heroes. Damian had trusted the other four men to arrange this meeting, so the details were up to them.

"Grandfather, you had said you would tell us more about the big struggle. Tell us that, please," one of the twins demanded.

"Oh, well… Um, okay, but that really comes later in the story so let me work it in after I talk about the Meeting of the Classes first, all right?"

"As you know, the *struggle*," he looks at Kaleb for acknowledgment, "began when hundreds of thousands were killed worldwide after the Martial Law was declared. I know I say Martial Law, and I say the New Norm. Well, to me, they are the same. They both have no good in store for the people. But, people were angry. They had lost their loved ones and seen their children, spouses, neighbors, parents, and friends suffer in front of their eyes. They felt helpless, and that only added to their rage. They knew they had to do something fast.

The four men, i.e., Arctay, Aelio, JW, and Wilgred, had arranged for the meeting in Damian's large backyard. The weather did its part perfectly to allow the outdoor meeting to be conducted hassle-free. Everything was preplanned and arranged with extreme caution so as to not raise any suspicions. They did not want any governmental authorities to find out about this meeting because no good would come of it. That could ruin our hero's plan, so secrecy was one of the main challenges that our heroes had to face to host this huge meeting. Damian designed his own cloaking apparatus to mask the activities of the day from surveillance. He tied the feed to his satellite to ensure against hacking, and his feed would be all anyone saw.

Our hero's house was enormous, and the backyard was even larger. They expected around 200 guests at the meeting, including leaders from Classes 3 and 4 from each state. The guests also included four Class 1 National leaders, so our hero had asked the four men who were managing the event to ensure that the hospitality was managed accordingly with paradisiac arrangements.

The grandkids squinted their eyes at the word 'paradisiac.'

"Paradisiac means like paradise." I clarified quickly.

The confusion cleared.

"We don't want to disappoint people, especially not the Class 1 leaders. So, we need to make sure that every arrangement is according to their standards of living. This is our first and only chance to make an impact on society through its leaders. If the people of the society extend their support to us and agree with our plan, then and only then can this plan work." Damian explained.

The meeting was destined for success. It would be held during the day and last into the evening. Before the adjournment, it would be clear that our hero had only two days to deliver what he had promised.

"Fellas," He opened the meeting with his four men two days before the actual meeting of the classes, "It is time. We are now able to complete our goal of addressing the recent wave of futile laws and inhumane acts."

"Is everybody clear about their assignments for D-Day?" He asked again.

"D, we have been over this. We even had tests and trials. We are ready, and we are doing this!" JW responded. Damian nods in assent.

"As you know, the tiny chips we created work using a timed process. It will help achieve the goal. This will be confusing to most, so we need to be careful."

He went on to discuss several details of how the disseminated information is to be worded and announced to the people to help them see the problem from their perspective and to help them gain confidence in the plan. The primary emphasis was kept by our hero on the wording of the idea because the wrong words can make even the best of the plans sound like crap. And our hero could not risk the people misunderstanding the plan or getting scared. It could ruin everything for them, and it was a huge responsibility to deliver the message as accurately as possible. So, guys, if you field any questions in your travels, we need to be on the same page.

Later that day, a few neighbors started to gather in the backyard, asking what the Meeting of the Classes was about. These people were neighbors who Damian talked to and trusted. He addressed them all together as a crowd and invited them to appear at the meeting.

"In a few days, people, as you know, Congress will vote on the stimulus checks to go out to the people. This is to be the biggest check ever to go to each citizen. There is a split in the positions, and the Speaker holds the deciding vote."

"Now, we have all suffered enough, some more than the others, but suffered, nevertheless. So, if we let the Speaker vote against us, the citizens of this country, then we are being clearly denied of all our rights. Now, that cannot go on. We have sacrificed enough, endured enough, and now, we must revolt."

Damian talked convincingly in a determined tone, and the crowd listened in awe as he explained the plan. "We all know his position, and we do not doubt his vote, right? So, with our plan, we can actually manipulate his thought process."

"You mean like subliminal messaging", asks Richard, his next-door neighbor to the right of Damian's spread.

"Exactly… but on steroids!

The crowd of neighbors looked at him with raised eyebrows and open mouths. Of course, not everyone had studied technology and electronics as our hero had.

"I encourage you all to attend the meeting to find out more, " deplored Damian. Wilgred added that this plan was unlike any other, and this move marks a huge step.

"Consider this our defense mechanism," Wilgred continued. "If we don't at least try to do this, then we have to give up our lives to a life of oppression. We cannot live like a herd of sheep being directed by them to fulfill their motives." They all agreed and became encouraged.

The attendees of the *Pow-Wow meeting* would include a lot of big shots. Some of these people were lawyers, doctors, educators, engineers, businesspeople, and whatnot. They were powerful, too, but their power was limited now that the governmental authorities had redefined their reach and implication of power.

Damian, our hero, wanted those influential people there because their support, financially and otherwise, could really strengthen their plan. Luckily, he sensed that most of them seemed very interested.

Damian set this meeting for one huge purpose: to give hope back to his community. And hope is such a strong motivator to allow people to keep going in their lives. Do you know how many people, especially in the prime of their lives, literally killed themselves simply because they had no hope left? Damian could not let this happen anymore.

He had a plan that he believed in, and he was confident of one thing: even if no one else believed in the plan, they believed in

Damian, and he believed it could at least give people the hope that something good was coming their way and that there is light at the end of this dark, long tunnel.

Damian's backyard was a virtual gala setting. A huge tent graced the south end of the enormous property. In it were accommodations for over 200 people. Air conditioners adorned the tent throughout. Speakers, a stage with a podium, refreshments, and what appeared to be tons and tons of preparation with the decorations, seating charts, and guides posted along with copies of the agenda. Damian kept secret the cloaking apparatus he had deployed. Using one of his own satellites, he could jam signals and mask the activities from any potential eavesdropper.

Damian confidently opened the meeting by saying, "I thank you all for coming today. Your time and efforts in the struggle that has engulfed us all are greatly appreciated. And I also hope the accommodations are to all your liking.

"It is through our combined efforts," Damian continued, "that we finally make a difference in the quality of life for all the world's citizens. And so, today, we are meeting to discuss ways to advance these efforts further. While we have many issues to address today, I want to later discuss your top challenges from a legislative perspective. I have decided to divide you into groups of ten, where you come up with two main challenges per group; Damian went on, "We will then discuss the results. More on that in a little while. Sound like a plan?"

No dissents.

The people listened attentively.

"Would anyone like to say something to the group before we begin?" He confirmed.

"Yes, I want to say something," says Antonio Bruno, the Rep from Italy. He rises in a tailored plaid suit so commonly found there and with his best broken English, says, "I want to express, on behalf of everyone here, the appreciation we share for our host today. A man who tirelessly works to see that there is justice in the world. A man I call a friend and a man we can all call our friend. Thank you, Mister Damian!"

Again, and in response to the cheers, a breach of his ever-present, stoic demeanor, a blush was noticeable on his face as he tried to suppress the smile that crept across his lips anyway.

With the 200-plus people gathered in Damian's backyard for the big day, they were told the plan as it was.

Damian, our hero, stood at the podium erected in his backyard. He stood in the center to head the meeting of the classes, and his four brethren sat around him as they normally did.

"My dear fellowmen and women, we are survivors. First of all, I want to thank you all for being here and for being strong enough to accept that there is still hope for all of us. My dear fellows, I will start by telling you that my friends here and I have a plan. We have an amazing idea that, if executed correctly, can free us from the injustice of the government. Do you believe that is possible?"

They listened to him, looked up to him, believed in him, and supported him faithfully as not only a leader but also as a friend. He continued to address the crowd.

"It was not long ago that the idea came to me. I was discussing some things – some technological topics – with my friends when it occurred to me that if there is some power, other than any divine powers, that has the ability to alter human behavior… it is either medicine or technology. Now, the idea we have is not medical in any way but is surely a medicine for the sick-minded and corrupted."

The crowd looked confused and curious, wondering what exactly the plan was. Damian did not enjoy beating around the bush, but he knew that he must first prepare the audience's minds to accept the plan, and that was what he was doing now. He wanted them to realize how trapped they were in the system of inequality, discrimination, and injustice and then understand that what our hero was offering was, indeed, the only solution.

"Among my peers, I once said, and now I repeat, that the only way that we can all have the right to live and live freely is to overturn the government. I said it as a joke at that time, but then I realized that really was the only answer to most of our problems: If we could somehow make each corrupt government official resign or change their positions, we could cleanse the entire country's system and start all over again. Fresh, new, and clean…."

The crowd listened to our hero talk, and they were still not sure what he was getting at. Some of them were enjoying the way he was building up the plot. In contrast, the others were simply impatient, occasionally calling out, 'How?' or 'What is the idea, D?'

Our hero decided it was time to tell them what the plan really was, but he did not want to reveal too much too soon. *Don't scare them off,* he thought to himself. Say it just the way you planned it.

Damian took out a package from an envelope. It was an electronic chip sealed inside a small plastic bag, but all the crowd could see was the plastic bag.

'What is that?' Someone from the audience asked as all of them were squinting their eyes, trying to see what was contained in the plastic bag and failing.

"To get straight to the point. A chip… an electronic chip, is what we're looking at." Our hero clarified. "We have created these tiny chips that can begin a timed process. That process can be programmed to help us achieve our goal."

There was a lot of questioning, confused, surprised, wide-eyed exchanges of glances among the 200 people gathered in Damian's backyard for the meeting of the classes. This was new for all of them.

"As I mentioned, our goal is to cleanse the government. I would like to emphasize that, please, do not mistake our plan for a quest for power or authority. No, we do not want that. We simply wish to live and let live, but that is too much to ask for with the current government. Don't you all agree?"

The people hooted in affirmation. This was the time to reveal the plan of action. They were all interested and accepting of using these chips.

"These are very powerful chips, and I have worked extensively on these to ensure that they do not cause any harm to the implanted person. And yet, these can change how that person thinks, behaves, and responds. Magical, isn't it?"

Damian could see that many of the people, especially of the upper classes, were nodding, impressed at the invention.

"Right now, that chip… It has been sent to the Speaker as ensured by our man, your son," Damian said, looking and gesturing at the Class 1 Rep from Northern California, "Simon, who works in the dining facility. Now, we only need to activate it, but the timing must be precise. Our own media campaigns combined with the power of this chip will be enough to get some long-wanted change."

Many of them responded with hoots and claps, while some of them raised questions, but one reaction was common: surprise.

"How do we know this will work? How do you know that things will get better?" One of the men asked after raising his weather-beaten hand. One could hardly tell if his hands were even clean, permanently stained from his life's work. He was probably a farmer by the look of his clothes that had non-removable mud and soil on them. These were the classes that were affected the most. They had suffered the most since the beginning, and if our hero was not trying to improve the situation, they would still be suffering because of the lack of financial authority and power they held.

"What do we ever *know?* We don't. We only plan, take action, and execute our plans to the best of our capacities. Of course, we all have the power to think and analyze, so take your time to think and analyze what seems right to you: Their unjust rule, or our smart plan?" Damian responded. They continued the discussion, and Damian fielded their questions very guardedly. He did not want to give out too much information.

"I understand that not all of you will completely understand the technical functionality of our plan, and that is okay. See, I could have done this independently and secretly, but I gathered you all here to prove something not only to myself but to you all as well: This meeting of the classes made you all forget about the class differences amongst you and got you to stand here in this ground, together, united, and equal. No longer is it Dreg of Class 4 standing next to a There from Class 1. No, we see two people sharing a common cause and here because they do stand together in that cause. Our opinions may differ, and our beliefs may be contrary at times, but this mission to cleanse the government and restore justice in this country is enough to unite us all as citizens or residents without any classifications based on our financial or familial backgrounds. Isn't that true?"

There was some silence; the people had just begun to realize that they had, indeed, forgotten about their differences. Yes, truly, some of the most senior or important personalities amongst the audience were given better seating arrangements than others at the meeting of the classes, but generally, Class 4 Dreg citizens were standing only inches away from Class 1 There citizens. They were all side by side, which was something openly discouraged and hated by the current government because they were readily playing the divide-and-conquer strategy.

"Understand this, my dear brothers and sisters, that our unity scares them. It scares them to death because when we are united, we are stronger than them, bigger than them, and have much more authority than them. All these years, they have been able to kill our children, our spouses, our families, and our friends because we were all scattered, but if you all support me in this plan's execution, we can save our country and even save the world."

Our hero's speech had motivated many of the people there who were otherwise hopeless and had accepted their tragic fate.

"When the project is done," Damian spoke to the many people at the meeting, "We should be able to bring a semblance of peace amongst the classes and between them and the government."

This was the ultimate goal. Our hero was not looking for power for himself. He did not want to become a leader or govern the country. While some people may have thought that he was doing this for his own political power, it was not so. Damian wanted peace for everyone, and that was only possible if the government would either be cleansed of the toxic people or the toxic mindset.

Following Damian's speech, Aelio ensured the meeting's attendees formed groups to discuss what problems they had faced or were struggling with so that the troubles could be addressed and prioritized based on their urgency and commonness. The people who had gathered there started forming subgroups. They were actively and eagerly discussing their issues. Some were talking about how their properties were taken away by the government to make 'public' facilities but were turned into private properties by lawmakers and the government thugs. Many of those people had managed to buy properties after spending their entire life savings. Sadly, no compensations were given to them by the government-backed home mortgage giants, Manny Ray and Louie Jack, the organizations created specifically for that purpose.

Much of the youth in our hero's backyard attending the meeting were concerned about their privacy.

"We are constantly in fear of being watched. Our personal conversations, data, everything is being watched even in our phone's most private folders!" One of the young attendees complained.

A woman in her 30s complained about how her husband was being blackmailed into carrying out some illegal work by a government authority.

"They can watch us through our phones!" She cried. "You know what they did?! They recorded me changing my clothes in my bedroom and told my husband, a federal employee with the Internal Revenue, that they would make the video go viral on public platforms if he did not obey their commands!"

Many people were suffering.

"And that same data is being used to manipulate us through their channels. They sell our personal data for their profits and whatnot." Another angry young man in his 20s added. They say it is for our national security. But we know it is much more. They don't need to spy on us through our goddamn cameras and mics to ensure national security when the most major threat is sitting on our nations' thrones!

The people were furious and frustrated, and that was a good sign. Do you know why?" "No, Grandfather, why?" Nubia's sweet voice asks. "Because people show their frustrated emotions only when they have hope. They complain only when they know that there might be a solution. Before this meeting and the revelation of Damian's plan, people had just stopped complaining. They had stopped getting angry and had become used to accepting whatever was being pushed into their lives. That was because they had not been heard when they had been angry earlier, so they resorted to just letting things be and going with the flow because they had become *hopeless*. But now, just after hearing out our hero's plan, their hopes had begun to return.

This would be the beginning of real change.

Damian had further reminded that everybody must stress the powers of their lobbyists every chance they get, reiterating that there are already ads, campaigns, and commercials in place to aid their efforts.

The meeting *was* a great success, and everyone had confidence in Damian. He promised he would come through, and he was always a man of his word. Damian valued one's word and insisted everyone working with him always keep their word.

Their chip was revolutionary, and they knew that if the government had gotten a grasp on it, they would 'enhance' it to achieve their evil goals and even weaponize it. That was not the purpose of its design – it was built for peace.

Damian is constantly reminded that there could be hideous charges invented against our heroes if the government got knowledge of their chips and that everyone must be extra careful.

At the same time as Damian spoke, JW noticed Wu Lin amongst the crowd. He quickly approached Damian and asked if it was a good idea to have her present, especially with their history. Our hero replied that she was present precisely because we could not trust her. Her being here was part of the plan.

"Don't worry, JW," Damian says as he lightly punches JW's chin with a smile. Little did JW know that Damian had already put a chip in Wu Lin and was now standing back and observing the results.

Wu Lin and Damian used to date earlier before our hero had married Rose and had a family. However, their relationship had ended abruptly when Wu Lin had betrayed Damian's trust. Not only was she cheating on him, but also stealing from him. He found out several reasons in the meantime to not trust her, including her leaking sensitive information from the military to a foreign government official. This official was misusing that information to blackmail some men. Since that day, Damian knew that Wu Lin was one of the corrupted people and was an active facilitator of the corruption at higher levels of the country's government.

When the idea had sprung in our hero's mind to create the revolutionary electronic chip, of course, it had to be tested before it could be implemented on such a high level practically. So, when he created the first chip, our hero shortlisted a few people on whom he could try out the product as an experiment.

He knew that nothing bad was going to happen to them health-wise, so he considered it not really an evil move. But, regardless, he knew that he could not attempt to control someone innocent just like that because then, what would be the difference between him and the government?

So, among the shortlisted people, he finalized two people based on two characteristics: They were both very manipulative, had somewhat influence in the society, and facilitated corruption on a bigger level.

Out of those two, one was Wu Lin, his ex-girlfriend, and one was an elderly man who was a very dishonest lawyer of considerable influence. Out of courtesy for the old man's age and his health, our hero chose to put the chip in Wu Lin as a test. If it worked on her, it would work on the actual targets, too. And, if it did not work on her, then our hero would know to make changes before he would implement the actual plan.

However, Damian chose not to tell his partners about it because he did not want them to be involved in the testing. He was not sure how they would feel about it, especially because they did not know the kind of woman she was. They did not know what she had done and how she was the right one for this experiment. All they knew was that she was an ex-girlfriend, and he did not want them to think that he was choosing her as the target out of spite.

"Won't your wife mind it, sir? She being here?" JW asked again, teasingly. He knew that our hero's wife, Rose, had an extremely negative vibe from Wu Lin, and she had often expressed that she wished that women like her did not live in the same society as theirs. Damian's friends would sometimes even tease him about it.

"Oh, she knows. I told her that they are all invited, and I could not personally discriminate here," Our hero gave an honest explanation. His wife wanted to be there, too, but she was busy in the kitchen overseeing the preparation of some snacks for the meeting's attendees that day.

"Grandfather, was she making food for 200 people all alone?" Nekiya asked innocently.

"No, of course not! Our hero and his four friends had all contributed and helped prepare everything with her before the meeting had begun. She was working with the staff to ensure everything was perfect. And they were not serving a lot; it was just a basic menu that could give the audience a warm farewell as the meeting closed.

Our hero was a very calculating man. He had logic and a valid reason behind everything. That is why he was content with himself. So, when he pretended to bump into Wu Lin at a coffee shop a month before the meeting of the classes, he put the chip in her cup of coffee that she was drinking, of course, without her knowledge.

After some days had passed, Damian had begun manipulating her responses to different situations through his computer. As planned, the chip was working and changing her mindset and thinking patterns altogether, so to test her, he started to strike up conversations with her occasionally in the neighborhood or elsewhere. Nothing life-changing– just small talk. During those small talks, he would ask her something about the injustice in the society or other questions about corrupted governmental acts casually, and she would answer against them. She would answer like a good person would. In fact, some of the responses were exactly how Damian had programmed them to be. So, that was his cue to call the meeting.

Now, if the chip was not working on her, she would have run to tell her partners in the government about the big meeting. Damian began to reflect on the meeting he had with his cohorts.

So, my children, how do you like the story so far?

"Awesome!" Said the grandchildren in unison, eager to hear about more details of the big meeting.

"Go on, grandpa," said one of the twins. The twins are one of the most talkative kids among my grandchildren, which makes them uniquely adorable, too.

"So, as you know, my dear grandchildren, the meeting of the Classes – the big meeting – was arranged to be at our hero's home." The story continues.

The world had seen its fair share of troubles. The New Norm or the New Normal, whatever conspiracies were being cooked up by the government, had put their people directly under the steam of their plans, and it was not going to be tolerated for too much longer. Of course, everyone had struggled in this cold, brutal war. It had taken a huge toll on everyone, from the shot callers in Class 1 down to even the lowest and severely compromised people that fell in the lower classes.

But the system was designed this way. It was designed to make people overstep their boundaries. It was made to manipulate situations and enforce people into conditions that could make it easier to eliminate them.

And, of course, when these tolls affected the most prestigious and powerful members of Class 1 to the point where it caused them to cross their boundaries or misstep, our hero and his fellows knew how to use this situation to the benefit of their cause.

Wilgred, the brilliant lawyer and one of the most loyal friends of our hero, was completely dedicated to the cause. He knew the shortcomings of the law, too. So, he identified the missteps by the Class 1 members, skillfully averted the newly enacted laws and got convictions on them.

It is important to understand that, again, our hero's plan was not to serve himself or his motives but to serve what was left of humanity. The world had changed, and not in a good way. It had *malfunctioned,* quite literally, because the human race was not supposed to deteriorate as it did.

"Then, what was it supposed to do, Grandpa? What was the human race made to do?" One of the lovely grandkids asked with innocent puppy dog eyes.

"Ah, that is a question that has still not been answered. SO many researchers, scientists, philosophers, and scholars have proposed reasons why the human race exists and what its purpose – or purposes – may be, but there is no definitive answer. You want to know what I think the answer is?"

"Yes, grandfather."

I think the answer is subjective. Each of us has a unique purpose of being alive, born, and even living the life we live. But yet, each of us is born in a family, a community, so our unique purposes are interlinked with those around us. I believe that the human race was made to do just this: live and help others live until the angel of death arrives and takes us away.

"Can I tell the angel of death not to come to take me, grandfather? What if I don't want to go with him?" A sweet child asked.

"Ha-ha! Okay, great thinking, little one! Well, when he comes, he comes. But let's not diverge from our story right now, eh?"

So, we were talking about the world and how it malfunctioned. Just like an information system, the world has several chips and circuit boards that help run it. Some of these circuit boards and other components can occasionally stop working or malfunction, which causes errors in the system. Hence, the point is that even if one or some components do not work properly, the entire system suffers, and the same analogy applies to the countries and governments of the world.

Our world was not so problematic – it had its problems, but none so bad that they could create a whole evil plan to wipe out humanity in their hunger for power. Their evil strategies were soon publicly viewed by the opportunistic acts of the world's leaders and how the public was always oppressed and suppressed, deprived of their basic rights, and stripped of their ability to live freely in the countries they paid their taxes to. It was just twenty years ago when the people of the world rejected what was being forced onto them.

They took off their blindfolds and started to see the world for what it had become, with the forced economic depressions constantly making lives miserable and the phantom pandemics killing millions across the globe. Even religion was forced, and the concepts of worship faltered, eventually turning the government leaders themselves into fake gods who wanted to control everything. So many changes were introduced one after another that the people could begin to see the direction they were being forced to walk in, and they did not like it.

Possession of cash and its transactions were all banned as crimes, and everything became more electronic so that it could be monitored, watched, and controlled by *them*. Then, the declaration of Martial Law was also recognized as being one of the root causes of all this chaos and damage that the people had to bear and pay for. The people had decided that there was no place for a silly law enacted by a supercilious, self-serving group of lawmakers long past their usefulness. Not now. Not anymore.

"Grandfather," Myell interrupted the story. "What does supercilious mean?" She asked with the same glow of curiosity that kids have – I don't understand why that twinkle dies out as we grow. Do we stop thinking? Do we stop being curious or interested?

"That means that they think themselves as better than other people – or think that they are the most superior, sweetheart."

People started to see the reality of the supercilious lawmakers because their laws served only classes 1 and 2 . What about the others? What about justice and equality? How is it fair if a criminal from Class 4 gets lifetime imprisonment for murder, but a Class 1 criminal gets acquitted for the same crime? Of course, Damian, our hero, had an eye for detail and would not follow the '*law*' like a sheep.

He knew that he needed to change what he could not accept, which is what the meeting was about. After the meeting was over, the attendees were served some snacks with juices before they left. Many of the attendees had personally approached Damian and our four side-heroes to greet them and tell them that they are doing a wonderful thing for humanity. Some presented their own ideas and questions regarding the plan. At the same time, some of the Class 1 reps even offered financial assistance or the use of their contacts if the need arises.

This was all that our hero expected of the meeting, and they were successful in it. The checklist in our hero's mind ticked off another milestone: Plan finalization? Check. Reveal plan to friends? Check. Reveal plan to classes? Check. Execution of the plan? That's the next box to mark off...

CHAPTER 7
THE NEW ERA

The plan that was going to bring about a revolution had begun from a mere conversation at a high school reunion, so if you think about it, many revolutionary ideas come into being only by discussions among people. For instance, my dear children, there might be the seeds of an idea in your head that you might not even be aware of, but those seeds might sprout and grow while you are talking to a peer about a relevant topic. That is how you discover your best ideas. That is why I say that humans are social creatures, and it is so important for each one of us to talk to others, to discuss, to express, so that we find ourselves among those conversations.

Unknown to most people, our hero, Damian, had developed a love affair with technology, and especially with nanometer (NM) technology. He knew the potential that this field held and the revolutions that it could bring, but he had not thought before his reunion just how important those conversations about technology could be. It was a stroke of luck that the conversations steered towards the potential implementations of nanotechnology, our hero's passion, and of course, given his knowledge on the matter, he had a lot to talk about.

He knew that the world had been using sim-sized integrated circuits of chips in their latest dosage of technology to the public, and he could tell that it was going to get more intricate and integrate further into our people's lives.

"What is nanotechnology, grandfather?" Nekiya asked.

"Nano means tiny! And technology is… well, technology. Uh, you can say that the smallest versions of technology like your mobile sim cards are a form of nanotechnology. Is that clear?"

"Like memory cards?" Another grandchild quickly gave a practical example.

"Exactly!"

So, anyway, the development of technology was seldom released to every geographic region at the same time. The distribution of these resources was done based on the mandates of the elite of Class 1. When an innovative technology was invented, it took about two years for its release and implementation around the globe, and this 1.5 NM technology was about to stir some things up. It allowed the development of a chip so small that it is tinier than a human blood cell and can house up to 20 billion transistors!

The grandchildren circled around me listened with utmost interest when the six-year-old Nekiya interrupted to ask, "What is a transistor, grandfather?"

"Hey, sweetie… Great question! A transistor is… like, a device used to control the electronic signals and even the power of something, for instance, another device. So, suppose you are working on your computer. In that case, all the electricity that powers it and the circuits are controlled by really tiny transistors or immaculate wiring. Those are the things that keep your computer running and allow you to play that favorite game of yours! Uh… what was its name again?"

"It is called 'A Wonderful Life,' grandfather!" The kids answered in unison, excited about naming their favorite video game.

"Oh, yeah. That is the one where you can decide where you want to go in life – uh, I meant the game. Right, kiddos?"

"Yeah," Nekiya assented.

So, anyway, back to nanotechnology: The introduction of the 1.5 NM tech allowed the government and the other power-hungry authorities to have the smallest chips and inject them into all citizens through different methods. They used those chips and delivered them inside the people's bodies through serums, vaccinations, or even meat processing warehouses and other products where genetically modified organisms are processed. Those chips were so small that you could not see them with the naked eye or even through most detection equipment. Their primary function was to disrupt the immune system.

That was a problem, but our hero had begun to see the solution in this. He saw the opportunity put forward by this and his own developed nanotechnology and devised a plan which he immediately started to put into action.

One year before execution, the plan was explained in the conference room in our hero's house, and when he had his crew sitting around the large table, he began:

"Gentlemen, we are about to embark on a mission that will revolutionize everything as we know it, but it all has to remain a secret. Whatever we are discussing today requires confidentiality at the highest level. I have very often emphasized that we cannot clean houses when the government is spreading more chaos. But, with the help of some hackers that are known to be highly skilled and reliable, I have got the idea that we can create a .5 NM chip that can house billions of transistors."

Damian waited to see the expressions of his crew members. They all seemed genuinely interested and impressed, but of course, they were curious to know the rest of the plan.

Our hero continued: "This technology gives us the ability to create a new class of circuits. We could create circuitry that could allow us to actually control individuals! Of course, the chips can be tracked, and through tracking their electrical circuitry for each individual, we can target specific people and control their actions."

"Control them how?" One of his crew members asked, not sure where our hero was going with this idea.

"We can activate certain areas of the human brain by using the circuits on those chips just like any other chips are able to control machines. You know, we can control people's moods, their tempers, and even manipulate their actions through an undetectable implant in their bodies."

"Grandpa, isn't that evil?" One of the twins asked.

"Hmm… depends on our hero's intentions, really. But I have a whole discussion planned about good vs. evil and right vs. wrong. It's a moral dilemma, and we'll get into it later in the story, all right? You need to know the full picture before deciding who is evil and who is not."

"Okay," she nodded.

Okay. So, this idea could give them immense power as long as the secret is never revealed. This was the plan, the idea. Damian decided to recruit the best hackers in the world who were known for some of the biggest hacks in their day.

"Some of them were in prison, so I – I mean, Damian negotiated their releases, and now, they will work with him. You will notice their files in front of you," Our hero conducted the meeting and gestured to his friends to open the files in front of them.

The first file was of Shin Shong. He was famous for successfully hacking the United Sovereigns Organization. Nearly every country in the world was affected by his hack.

Wilgred smiled when he saw this file, "Yeah, easy dismissal for us! I remember that one! They thought we did it!" He added.

"Yep, then there is another man known as Ray Ray. He had masterfully hacked several countries' Departments of Defense."

Countries everywhere were scrambling to adjust their then-compromised defense systems.

Then, there was Ervst Makken's file. He had created a deadly virus that infected 20 percent of the world's computers by continuously resending itself automatically to the top fifty contacts from the hosts' address books. That was a very smart hack that forced two of the world's tech giants, Orange and Biggirl, to temporarily shut down operations worldwide.

"The next file on your desks is of Illya Zangerski," Damian stated as his crew members opened it.

"Of course, the person who hacked the gaming system used by the government."

"The government played games?" One of the grandchildren asked, surprised.

"Ha-ha, no, no. The government basically created a network for youth – uh, of people aged up to 40 years old, actually, where they could electronically connect a specifically designed box to any monitor and play interactive games, like the one you people play, *A Wonderful Life*."

The network also allowed them to watch movies and make video calls in addition to playing video games. But the problem with this was that these games were really violent. You might not know it yet, kids, but violent media and games are linked to several psychological issues. People develop aggression, anxiety, and violent personality traits as a result of constant exposure to these games and movies that normalize murder, bloodshed, and crimes.

Ultimately, our hero could tell that the games were accountable for the ability of so many young people to go around killing sprees and committing senseless crimes, which clearly showed the frustration and rage built up inside them. So, well, they would drink the Kool-Aid, so to speak, and completely bought into those networks and boxes but as a friend of mine used to say, "I ain't picking up what you are laying down!"

Trust is earned, not bought or sold. So, with these games and other media so integrated into the youth's life, the government had successfully desensitized them to the very thing that happens every day now, i.e., the constant struggle, the cold-hearted wars, killings, terrorism, and it is a long list of things that are not normal.

"Mr. Illya never liked the direction in which our youth and gaming industry was headed and was immediately on board with our plan. He was the easiest one to recruit," said Damian to his fellows.

Then, there was Aliya Shebaa. The beautiful, alluring, brilliant Aliya was able to breach and totally compromise the world's largest credit bureau and did some amazing damage. See, that's the thing, you might think about just how much wrong these people were doing, but you do not know their intentions yet, and neither are you aware of what was going on at the other end of the picture, so don't judge just yet. "But grandfather, you always told us that there is woe ahead for people that call good evil and evil good. How do we know if something is evil or good in the world today? I just don't get it." "Again, there are clearly evil deeds and some in question. Based on the principles I have tried to instill in you all, I trust you to make the decision that benefits you most. Remember, the needs of the many outweigh the needs of the few or the one. "Is that from an old Star Trek movie, grandfather?" I am not sure, but it does seem to fit here, right? "Yes, grandfather, it makes sense, but I can still see having a tough time deciding whether what I am doing is good or evil" I can only say, trust your training and your heart.

So, our hero had recruited some remarkable minds and created a skilled team. With this illustrious group, our hero had the ability and power to control people's minds and lives. That is how far technology had come! People could literally be turned into robots with a simple injection of these nanochips. The beauty of the chip is that it can be ingested or injected. Special properties in the chip allow it to be 'magnetically' attracted to its target area. That technology took quite a while to develop. But the hard work and diligence proved worthwhile. The trials and the innovative technology proved it was going to work. Damian and his crew patiently awaited D-Day.

Thursday had arrived, and the upcoming vote for the stimulus checks for citizens was scheduled as the main item. Many people, including Mister Donnelley, thought that it was unwise to pass the bill stating it would take money from cities and states suffering from the effects of their changes in governance.

People are weird with setting priorities. And, dear children, you must learn to set your priorities right. Financial reform and fiscal responsibility were the government's mantra at the time. They did not care if the non-passage of this was to the deprivation of citizenry.

Regardless, Mr. Donnelley had the deciding vote in the group, where they were as divided as anything. It was a shame that they had at last resorted to this, but it was necessary as per their mindsets and priorities.

When Thursday arrived, Damian anxiously awaited news of the vote's result. His man in the session immediately reported to him the good news! It worked! Donnelley had cast a vote to pass the bill as per our hero's plan, and this, my dear grandchildren, was the beginning of a new era. Yes, there were plenty of legislators that wondered why he would reverse his position at the last minute. He had done it before. Mr. Donnelley had no transparency about his actions and was known for changing his mind and voting at the last minute. This was part of Damian's plan. While it would be questioned, it would not be disputed once his vote was cast.

As Damian had planned, the nanotech chip was delivered to Donnelley, and with its success, he had influenced even the top members of the government. Of course, though, there was going to be a tremendous price for this power that he held now. However, his most major concern was now to keep this technology and plan a secret from the corrupt, weaponizing government. Or else, the so-called 'businessmen' would jump at the opportunity and sell it to the highest bidder.

"But, Grandfather, there are so many terrible people in the world. How would it be possible for our hero to protect his secret?" Mequella was quick to identify a question before the story proceeded.

"Well, that's quick thinking, Mequella. Very good. Okay, so the first thing our hero did was that he made sure that only a limited number of people knew about the plan in the first place. Obviously, the fewer, the better. Then, as time and the plan proceeded, along with cleverly planned misdirection, he kept his secret safe from those that he could not trust."

"Misdirection? What kind of misdirection did Damian use?"

The grandchildren were taking a good interest in the story. Their intriguing questions were proof of their curiosity.

"Hmm… Our hero had a lot of friends in each Class. Then, of course, he was the Leader of Class 2. A position he held not as a member of the Class. Damian's wealth and status easily put him amongst the *There*'s in Class 1. But his generosity, popularity, and capabilities chose a different path for our hero. He became the voice of Class 2 and an advocate for all people. With so many people aspiring to a higher class, Damian took it upon himself to bridge the gaps between the classes. Understand and communicate the plight of each class and try to unite them.

His lobbyists included a variety of people, including the most skillful and prominent poets, writers, and journalists of the time. You know the deal with artists, right? They have a different kind of charm. A charm Damian would use to present the thoughts and struggles of each class."

Damian's lobbyists were able to charm their audiences with their street talks, engagements and through what they wrote. Of course, they were very skilled with their words, and they even presented their artful words in the Halls of Congress. Their words invariably had a meaningful impact on their audiences, and they convinced the people to consider options other than those of doom. Or at least, doubt had entered their minds, providing a much-needed window for their plan. Should is a weird word, by the way. What you think someone *should* do is normally based on your own beliefs, so that is subjective. Psychology 606, basically!

While the super chip was already at work, the moving words of our hero's lobbyists were effective enough to change anyone's mind, even the minds of the most powerful people. A sort of anti-propaganda plan. So, people could tell that these artistic thinkers were changing the minds of the many. No hint of a super chip. See, now that's clever.

Remember about the patents, copyrights, and permits that I told you about earlier? When these things were introduced, they ensured that each of them depicted a completely different purpose. Obviously, the only way to do that was to know all the effects of the chip or other invention. Not unlike the pharmaceutical companies who know the side effects of a drug, revealed them confidently, and still sold billions, especially because some drugs that have positive properties seemingly outweigh anything negative. So, you see, my dear grandchild, it was all a big mind game.

But it was a very cleverly planned mind game. One could not tell what was going on unless they really dug in order to make any connection there. The government did what it was going to do, regardless. It snooped around for months for a clue but could not come up with anything. Damian and his gang actually built the items for which their inventions were designed and sold them successfully, too, and not even the members of the Lower Classes could tell that something fishy was up. No meeting, class, or people were aware of the big plan or how it related to the revolution and the new era. Not yet. No, believe it. He was taking every possible precaution. Damian knew he could only trust just so many people. As he would reveal the plan to more folks, he ensured that everything up to that point was secure. No loose ends!

"Oh, that makes sense," one of the lovely grandkids, Khandi, popped in. "In those old cartoon movies that you let us see, Grandfather, I remember that there was one time… No, wait, it's maybe all the time, the theme was to fight fire with fire and keep your friends close and your enemies closer. And, oh! It was also prominent that good always triumphs over evil!" She proudly added.

"Whoa, that is some very impressive takeaway, sweetheart. Look at you! I think you interpreted it well."

Okay, so, you see now what the plan was? The idea that our hero had come up with marked the beginning of a new era. The oppression and suffering at the hands of the power-drunk authoritative figures were no longer acceptable. It could be changed with our hero's idea and his plan's implementation.

Whether it was the right thing to do or not, don't get too deep into those thoughts until you have heard the full story. There was a lot going on, a lot that our hero had seen happen around him, and he was not one to give in to corrupted systems and sit and watch as the villains of the story would take over and rule. The goal was to ensure that the goals of the evil governors were not achieved, and for that, our hero knew exactly what to do.

He took something that he loved, i.e., nanotechnology, talked about it to his friends, and realized that his passion could turn into a revolution.

CHAPTER 8
THE REVOLT

The plan for the New World or the New Norm was in place by the government. When the government declared the pandemic, they used the press extensively and a lot of mind games. Seemingly, nothing bad was going on. It's a virus spreading crazily around the world, and evidently, the government is doing its best to try to protect us. Until all at once, they distract the masses with a so-called great human-interest story, such as the assassination of a world leader who they killed and fill the headlines. This move would belie the seriousness and severity of the change caused by the pandemic.

That only gave them more space to expand the set of restrictions and impositions while masking their hostile strategies behind the idea of protecting the people. A new set of laws and executive orders were passed to strip the citizens of more and more rights. They tried to control literally everything from where you go, who you visit, who you live with, and how you live.

Rights of the masses were taken away: Rights that allowed folks to gather in large groups, whether for protest or entertainment. Rights that prevented folks from adequately providing for their families. Laws were passed that allowed corporations to provide less than a living wage to their employees.. Restrictions on the amount of food one can purchase at a time. Restrictions on travel and the purchase amount for gasoline for vehicles, generators, and other devices. There were even restrictions on the people's ability to have children. While this was not new, countries around the world were practicing this for years. Now every country had similar laws.

But that was not all of it. The government was not satisfied with this amount of control over their people and wanted more. You see, my dear grandchildren, that is the thing about power and money – the more you have, the more you want. These two aspects, usually interlinked, are the world's worst drugs. Their greed only increases, and the deeper one falls into their addictions, the lesser they are able to *live* with humanity.

Regardless, the people who were ruling the countries were already so drunk of their powers that they could not stop trying to control people – trying to become *gods*. The restrictions extended further to control even the most personal of their life's aspects, like limiting the number of children a family could have. Our hero had lived a freer life when he was younger and had not seen such restrictions in his youth, so when these new rules were imposed on the people, it was more noticeable for people like him to see how times were, in fact, changing for the worse.

Damian had seen the prominent shift in the way business was being conducted at all levels, especially because he had retired from the military, the federal agency, and the corporate realms.

The geopolitical scenarios of the world were also changing. That just means the politics of the world, guys. Countries were at odds with each other more than any time in history and had begun to close off their borders, restricting departures and arrivals at their airports as well. So, obviously, tourism and other industries took a major hit as people could rarely travel. So many families suffered at the hands of the so-called pandemic because of the border restrictions. Can you believe my grandchildren, that husband and wife, and even parents and kids were kept apart by these border closures? Lives changed drastically at this time.

Long gone were the days when there was far less outward discrimination. And, while the discrimination was horrible enough to have folks hate others based on things like their skin color, their individual beliefs, or even their handicapped bodies, it was so difficult to live with any aspects that were "different" or "unacceptable" to these hate-filled people.

I would never encourage hate, my dear grandchildren. You must all respect and love everyone regardless of their class, background, skin color, gender, or any other difference. Do not discriminate among any of your friends, and never think of the superiority of one gender or race over another.

But, my dear children, there are certain things to hate. I do not encourage hatred, but I hate injustice. I hate people who cook up evil thoughts and plans against others with evil deeds and intentions. Yet, because we are each on our own journey, the crossing of our paths does not have to be confrontational. It does not have to be with malice. Do you all understand what I am preaching here? A wise man once said, 'Not that I speak of respect of want, for I have learned in whatsoever state I am, therewith to be content.' This simply means that we sometimes want more than our share and have trouble being satisfied with what we have. Do not covet, my grandchildren.

"Yes, grandfather!" The kids responded altogether.

There is an old phrase of a language that is long lost, at least unspoken now for over 2000 years, that goes, 'Salute plurimam dicit. Sivules, bene est, ego valeo.' It means: 'Many greetings! If you are well, then that is good, and I am well, too.' Think about it!

The revolt was the worst time for our hero. There was so much going on around him that he wanted to change. He had a plan that he knew would work out well, but he also understood that it could have severe consequences if their plan backfired or if he got caught.

One day, while our hero was going on a walk around the city to observe his final findings before the plan was to be put into action, his wife had left for the sanctuary. She often went there, and Damian was particularly concerned about this because while sanctuary leaders were actively spreading the message of standing up for your rights, they were attracting the wrong kind of attention from the government.

Damian tried to talk to Rose about it, telling her that these meetings were one of the riskiest activities these days. She argued that she could not sit back from the Lord's work because she was not a coward.

"It is The Most High's soul that I have been given, and if He takes it, I don't mind."

She was right. Our hero was proud of her for not being a coward, but because he loved her so much, he did worry for her.

Anyways, these were some of our hero's concerns. Coming back to his plan: Damian wanted to reform as many people in the government as possible and convince all the others to resign. It was a form of cleansing of the system. According to his plan, he was determined, to begin with, the Senate Majority Leader, Butch Donnelley.

"Why him, grandfather?"

"Well, for starters, he had been a very disagreeable man whose sole purpose had apparently been to wreak havoc between the two major political parties."

By doing this, Donnelley was continuing in his power while strengthening the divide and, as a result, crippling the nation's progress. Furthermore, he had backed the country's leader in his mission of decimation. Then, when the pandemic completely overwhelmed millions of lives in every way, he refused to provide any financial relief to the country's people when they were relying on his consideration.

All those people depended on the government as their last resort to take care of them, but all they got in return was a long wait in vain.

Our hero said, "If we attack Speaker Donnelley's anterior insular cortex, that specific part of the brain controlling his emotions, we could effectively manipulate his ability for empathy. We do not need to rely on proximity for this to work, though. A range of 2,500 miles will do the trick."

The Idea was brilliant. It would work like a charm, and reversal of position will then become commonplace for this leader or anyone else in opposition. The hero had achieved this goal, as you might recall, by getting the chip delivered into the Senator through Simon, the hero's guy who worked in their dining facility.

Damian sat his fellows around him to explain the next step of the plan. "The next target is the country's Attorney General. You all know who that is, and we plan on making his transformation to be right out the door! If everything goes as planned, he will abruptly resign after we zap his amygdala and insula."

The idea behind this target's chip implantation was to give him immense guilt through his dosage. Coupled with our media campaigns directed at the Attorney General, that should be enough to make him resign quite unexpectedly. His crime, you ask? Well, let me tell you, dear children, when someone does something wrong, and you support or facilitate them in the crime, you automatically become a partner in crime. For that reason, you are equally responsible for the negative effects of those actions, even if you did not directly do the crime yourself. Hence, the Attorney General was also an indirect criminal as he was responsible for protecting a President who did not care a single ounce about protecting his people.

Our hero knew that his plan was going to make an impact on a massive level, so he had addressed his partners before the big meeting of the Classes, remember? He had said, "I will caution you, fellows, that if the government ever gets wind of our activities, we are finished. That is why we cannot tell the men and women in the meeting tomorrow just how we plan to execute our plan." This implies just how top-secret this mission was.

"What about the revolt, though, Grandfather? You said you would tell us more about that." One of the grandchildren said.

"Ha-ha, yes, we are steering towards that now, impatient little children!"

So, as I told you earlier, the big meeting of the classes was held after many people had died once Martial Law was declared. And this does not even include those who died from the virus that was borne or developed, or whatever.

People had become increasingly fed up with the mistreatment, the poverty, and all the inhumane acts. This was sparked when a citizen of a small town in the Light Continent was killed as collateral damage.

"What does collateral damage mean, grandfather?"

"It means an acceptable loss. Don't ask me how to determine what an acceptable loss is. I can never agree that people should be killed, especially like that. It was an 'accident' that happened during one of the government's operations."

But that did not go unnoticed by the people. The townsfolk were enraged and stood up because he was a leader in the village. Soon, similar incidents occurred in countries all over the world, and the word got out, which caused the movement to begin. Of course, all the government killings of citizens had already created a boiling point unlike any other before.

This would have been dismissed as isolated or not significant. With conditions as bad as they were worldwide, though, it was hard to cover up the murder of a real freedom fighter. As other freedom fighters were killed around the world, it became time to stand up. Damian used his informing newsletter that circulated around the globe to combat all the fake news being reported by the big propaganda machine known as the media. He had to resort to a modified form of analog faxing signals to spread his word about the movement.

This movement was what was called the revolt. Initially, acts were conducted covertly, but then the movement became open and real to the people. *'How much is enough? We will not take this any longer'* became their battle cry.

There were rallies of people with signboards held up in the air with demanding slogans. There were isolated cases of villagers seizing control in areas where the atrocities were really high. Government intervention sparked more rage in some areas. They would gather outside churches, government offices, and even on roads, chanting and yelling that enough is enough.

Unfortunately, the government only made things worse by sending the police to beat these people and disperse these crowds. (Thankfully, immediate executions were a thing of the past at that time .) It was, again, a tactic to scare people by treating them like animals so that they would not dare to speak up again. Any sort of gatherings started to attract police raids in which people were beaten, injured, or as bystanders, arrested for no reason – talk about a blind legal system! There were no laws to restrict the authorities and countless laws to restrict the unarmed, unharming citizens.

Such was a common occurrence. During one of the raids, a worship center near our hero's house was raided. There was a discussion going on there about the revolt and how the Lord encourages us to fight our battles against the unjust. Damian's wife was there that day, and she never returned home alive. She was to be the keynote speaker at the event. When Damian found her amongst the burnt ashes where once stood a sanctuary, she had a bullet wound through her chest. Some of the witnesses said that she must have gotten caught in the crossfire between the police and the congregation's guards. A gas main was hit and the ensuing blast wiped out nearly everyone and everything in a 200-meter radius, police and civilians alike.

Nevertheless, our hero was left alone and devastated. His wife had died in the revolt. For some days, he felt demotivated about the whole plan because his first motive was to make the country safer for his family. Many expected Damian to use all his power and influence to catch these scoundrels. The ones who took his world away. But Damian had another plan. He would not use any of his resources. He would do it alone. With the help of one of his own satellites, he was able to get surveillance info on the perpetrators, track them down to exact his justice on each one, individually. Six men in total. Six acts of retribution!

"Oh no… That's so sad…." One of the twin girls said, pouting. But what happened to the six men, Grandfather?" "Yeah, tell us, Grandfather."

Well, our hero waited patiently for 2 months studying their habits once he located them. He then lured them to the same hotel where they often met. He had put a chip in each of them with the help of a woman he used to put it in their drinks. Once at the hotel room, already stocked with swords and pistols, the chips were activated and the men destroyed each other. Not one was left alive. The chip gave their brains a message that the chemical serotonin was really high and it began dumping like crazy until it destroyed their prefrontal cortexes and they went crazy. This is the way our hero saw it in his head time and time again. And, everything worked up until they were in the hotel room. Before our hero could activate the chips, there was an explosion! Someone sent a grenade into their room. Someone had beaten our hero to his revenge. Was this good or bad? Apparently, these guys were hated by more than just Damian. Our hero was nowhere near the scene as he relied on his surveillance equipment to show him what was happening so no suspicion could be cast on him." "So, Damian did not have to take their lives? " asks Khandi. "No, baby. Fate or luck caught up with them. And it is a good thing because Damian would have to live with the taking of their lives. He could never get over it as it went against everything he believed in. I guess anger from loss can make people do things they probably would not do otherwise.

"Grandfather, didn't Grandmommy get shot while at Worship, too?" One of the children asked. . Damian looked at his group and thought carefully before answering. He knew if he said too much, they would be curious about whether he, too, set out for revenge. He was not prepared to discuss this with them. Not just yet. But he knew he would tell them. Instead, as he prepared to answer, he gave them all the look that instantly said, 'Now listen and ask no questions'.

He then proceeded to say: She was… Many people died during the revolt, my dear kids, like your grandmother and like our hero's wife, and that is why our hero knew that his wife's death was now all the more reason for him to fight back harder and stronger. This was now personal for him, and he was enraged. For the next few months, Damian worked on his plan. He had gotten closure on his wife's tragic death with the actions taken on those six. He was now ready for the plan. He knew he could not, would not fail!

At long last, the aggressions and skirmishes slowed. The movement had not stopped, but it did not need nearly as much focus as before. It became a policing force for occasional irregularities.

Now, my dear grandchildren, times improved a lot. The Treaty of Pontiac, once ratified, made an enormous impact on the way the governments treat its citizens. For months, there remained skirmishes when extreme disagreements occurred or other times when vigilantes took action because of a rogue official that did not get the message, but the situation had now calmed down to a good extent. The government murders had finally subsided, thanks to resistance movements cropping up everywhere. One of the only things remaining was to address the harmful legislation to which all the people were subjected and the reversal of existing or outdated bad laws.

"So, grandfather, what did you do during the revolt?" Nekiya asked.

"I promise to tell you that, but some time later. I will tell you at our get-together next month. For now, all I can tell you is that I fought for what I believed in. Do not let me forget when we meet at the next month's gathering," I said sternly in a way they all recognized. There were shrugs and 'ughs' but assent by all.

CHAPTER 9
THE MORAL DILEMMA

So, kids, do you remember the high school reunion of our hero? It was right after that reunion that our hero had gotten his brilliant idea. One important thing about our hero was that he believed in success more than anything, and when his intent was right, he did not care much about anything else. Yes, our hero had a solid plan, and he did not dare to stop and think whether it was the right thing to do.

Is it ethical? Is it morally correct? He did not think of things that way. It was the only thing to him and the only solution, and as long as his conscience was clear and his motives were good, he did not question his plan. That's the thing, my dear grandchildren: most of us get stuck into an endless spiral of what's right, what's not, and that stops us from getting into places and from doing anything new, daring, or revolutionary. That is because we define right and wrong based on what the society says or thinks. But remember, just because 50 billion flies eat dung does not make it right for everyone! "You know Grandfather, sometimes I think anything could come out of your mouth," Rahij smartly says. "True, True. But would you have it any other way? Grandfather responds.

Now, you tell me, who decides what is right and what is wrong? You might not know it yet, but I believe there is no right or wrong. Every action is judged by intentions, and only intentions can be good or bad. So, when you have an amazing plan, and the idea of its moral standing or ethical righteousness stops you, take a second to think what your intentions are and then take a leap. Otherwise, if everyone follows only the boundaries defined by society's scale of right and wrong, there will never be an out-of-the-box idea or a revolution.

Anyways, you know what Damian's plan was. He was going to use the beautiful little chips to change how the *leaders'* minds worked to ensure that justice was served to all. His intention was to save the society from the evil leaders that were serving only themselves while making their people suffer. Hence, his intentions were clear of any negativity.

"But, grandfather," asks Mequella, "He wanted to control people's minds, right? Is it right to control the minds of people in real life?" She raised a valid question that I was impressed about; raising questions is a sign of a witty mind. Only a wise person asks questions and requires answers before believing anything. A foolish person only follows what they are told blindly – the lack of thought itself makes a person's mind redundant.

"Remember when I told you about my Uncle Art? He instinctively knocked that man out using brute force. Like I said earlier, it may not have been the best solution for that situation, but Uncle Art was deeply convinced and believed that this was the right course of action. You have to consider nature and your roots." I explained.

"Do you guys think that man got the message?"

"When he woke up, I'm sure everything was clear to him," says Myell.

Nature has built us this way. In fact, you will find many instances of varied species taking action for their survival. For instance, take the lion: a grown male lion will 'invade' a lion's pride or family. He will kill the leaders of that pride and eat their young cubs, and then, he will mate with the females of that pride for one purpose, i.e., to continue his bloodline. That is for his bloodline's survival. At the same time, the leaders of the pride do not just sit around and let this all happen. This is his family, and he will and must do what it takes to protect his way of life. A battle follows, and the winner takes all.

Now, I know what you are thinking, but for an animal that is the king of its kind, there is an extraordinarily strong urge to ensure that he can continue to survive. Is it right for the lion to kill and eat the innocent babies to eliminate all competition? Is it wrong to fight to the death for yourself, your family, and your way of life? Of course, many people would base the answer on their beliefs and say that this is a terrible act that should never be justified. But they have to remember, the lion is only doing what a lion does. As people, we do what people do. And that, my dear grandchildren, all centers around survival. Eventually, an oppressed people will instinctively stand up against continued oppression. I think it must be a very slow, evolutionary process because it seems to have taken a very long time.

But is it wrong for the lion to act on his instincts to survive, or should he just say, "Oh, well, I lose, and I guess I will just scooch over to this corner, sit here and die?" No, our brains are not wired like that. Talking about brains, let me tell you something remarkably interesting: our minds think in the most effective manner when we are in survival mode, i.e., when someone tries to harm you or if the situation is against you, your senses are automatically heightened, and you begin to think more clearly, better.

Nevertheless, what we base our beliefs on is rooted in what our experiences and our parents/guardians or even friends teach us. All people teach their young ones to love and hate, but what to love and what to hate is the key, my dear grandchild. Hate injustice. Hate greed. Hate malice.

"What is malice, Grandfather?" Rahij Jerlissa asked quickly as the story went on.

"Hmm… Let me see how to put this… Malice… it is the intention to do evil, dear. Does that seem understandable?"

"Yes, grandfather," she nodded.

The key is not just being convicted of your beliefs. One can believe anything if properly motivated for it. If you are raised to believe that certain folks are subservient to you, for any reason, everything you do will be based on that belief, even if you think that you have no such discriminatory thoughts. No, you must understand what to believe in, and this whole thought process goes on in our subconscious minds.

"What is the subconscious mind, grandfather?" A curious one's voice echoed in the group.

"Uh, that's a complicated term for you, dears, but let me explain it as simply as I can: The subconscious mind is a mind inside your mind that determines how your active mind thinks. So basically, any fears or feelings you have are in your subconscious mind, but any worded thoughts in your head are in your active mind. Does that make sense to you?"

"Sort of…"

"Ha-ha! Never mind. Don't get too worked up about that. You will learn as you grow what that is."

That is why I want to give you some food for thought. You have to always consider the consequences of your actions because, as Newton said so many, many centuries ago, every action has an equal and opposite reaction. There are rules and laws that we must follow. There are some set boundaries that must not be crossed. For instance, murdering someone can never be justified, regardless of the reasons or the situation. But, self-defense is another matter. There are possessed and demonic people that sometimes cannot be stopped any other way.

You hope to never be in such a situation, but we live in a different world, and anything is possible.

"Now, who can tell me what a moral dilemma is?"

D3 promptly and quite robotically said, "A moral dilemma is a conflict of morals where you are forced to choose between two or more options, and you have a moral reason to choose and not choose each option." "Wow, D, what did you do? Look that up online? Sounds like you read it word for word", he teases.

"Wow, that is quite impressive. You seem to be thinking very creatively, Damian! Now, can someone give us an example of a moral dilemma?"

Silence ensued. Crickets chirped in silence for what seemed to be an eternity. I waited for an answer from the children. Then Rowena says, "It is like, knowing you can only save one, deciding whether to save a dog or your sister from a fire."

One cannot be cruel to animals, but you cannot let your sister burn either, hence, a moral dilemma."

"Very good, Dear. Exactly. Although, I don't believe too many folks would save the dog."

"Yeah, they would *really* have to hate their sister to do that!" jokes D3.

The group of grandchildren laughed.

"Now, who can tell me what you have learned so far about deciding what is right based on your morals?"

"Grandfather, we have learned that morals are subjective and that you decide what is right or wrong based on your intentions," The twins enthusiastically added, completing each other's sentences.

"Very good. Now, let me tell you a few more things about the moral dilemmas we face in life, my dear grandchildren, because this is one of those topics that one can discuss about their whole life and not come to a conclusion. Can anyone tell me why?"

The group of grandchildren circled around me just watched me with big, blank eyes.

Okay, let me tell you, kiddos, why. Remember, morals are subjective and vary from individual to individual, so I may opine that something is morally correct, but another person may completely oppose me on this matter. So, really, unless you have some super good persuasion skills, people rarely change their morals and values.

For instance, let me ask you this: Will I be a good grandfather if I yelled at you all?

"No, grandfather!" They all sang in unison.

Exactly! But I will be a good grandfather if I buy you candies every day?

"Yes, grandfather!" They all sang together again.

There, you have it. Now, I believe that I would not be a good grandfather if I bought you all candies every day because candies are bad for your health! So, my moral values tell me that I should care for your health more than your little wants that I would love to fulfill otherwise. Now, those are *my* morals, and they decide which course of action I take.

Now, let's take a look at the bigger picture: People's morals are decided not just by the society they live in but also by the experiences and teachings they are exposed to in their societies. Suppose a person lives in a home where they witness domestic abuse commonly. In that case, they are likely to eventually become abusers when they grow up, too, because, for them, it would not be an immoral thing to do. In fact, if you ask them, they will justify it with all kinds of reasons they have made up in their minds to *believe* that abusing someone is morally correct. This includes the line, 'I just couldn't help myself,' or my personal favorite, 'The devil made me do it!'

"Grandfather, what about us fighting? I fight with Damian all the time," Damian III's younger sister pointed out.

"Ah… well, you shouldn't fight with anyone. Not even with

your siblings, but let's face it: when you are kids, it is okay to have little conflicts among brothers and sisters. That is the thing that you will miss the most when you grow into adults and live separately."

"So, I *should* fight with him? Is it morally correct?" She reconfirmed as D3 gave her a threatening look.

"No! No, of course not! You should not, but if you do, it is not a huge crime. You're kids right now, you play, you cry, you fight – those are all simply different ways that you learn and grow."

Now, talking about fights, you must all also learn how to pick your fights.

CHAPTER 10

THICK AIR

Conflicts are a part of life, but what battles you pick determines what battles you win. Hence, it is especially important to understand who to fight, what to fight for, and when to fight.

Our hero, Damian, knew that his mission to save humanity was stemming from a conflict: a conflict of opinions, mindsets, strategies, and most importantly, priorities. And even though he knew that he was getting up against the most powerful rival there could be, i.e., the government, he was not afraid because he knew what his fight was for. He knew what he was standing up for.

My dear grandchildren, life presents several challenges, many of which are governed by our motives. If our motives are clear and defined, it is not too difficult to be focused on what matters. Many times, people get lost in the unnecessary elements of a conflict, e.g., ego, hatred, etc. None of that matters. What matters is that you remember what purpose you are fighting for, and if that purpose is not ill-intentioned, it should be achieved.

Our hero knew what he was doing and why – that is why we call him our *hero*. He also had the support of his fellow men because they were all united in that purpose. So, my dear children, whenever you find yourselves in a conflicted situation in life, evaluate your position: see where you stand, what you believe in, what is right and wrong, and what you are fighting for.

Now, so far, you know that our hero's plan was being executed just as he wanted. So far, I have not told you about the conflicts and obstacles that slowed him down or got him into demanding situations, right?

"Right, grandpa!" The kids said in unison.

Good, that is because I wanted to tell you about the conflict separately. I need my grandchildren to understand that every relevant story is made from a conflict and that every journey you will make in life will have at least one obstacle or conflict. That is what makes life interesting, even when you think that it is difficult.

When our hero had conducted the big meeting of the classes, there were many people there, as I already mentioned. But were they all trustworthy? Maybe... Maybe not. Like Wu Lin, there were many others who were among us but were working secretly for the government or for other governments but were involved in illegal or unethical conduct, nevertheless. They were the traitors and the secret information traders. In fact, they were making money and reaping benefits off of the government by being traitors to us at times, and then going around ratting out about our government's activities to foreign governments to get money from them as well! Now, this is what you can clearly identify as an immoral thing to do. Remember our story about the moral dilemma?

"Yes, grandfather!"

Very good. Now, back to our hero's story...

Our hero, Damian, was incredibly careful about ensuring that his idea or his plan was not leaked to the government because, of course, if they knew, they would not let him live or go on with his plan as he had wanted.

Unfortunately, among the people gathered in Damian's backyard, there were two who were still the government's secret agents: Wu Lin and Chris Winterson. Damian had already injected a chip into Wu Lin, so she was not much of a threat, but Chris Winterson's ties with the government were kept so secret that our hero and his men had little idea what danger could fall upon them.

They had carried out the meeting as planned and had gone about with business as usual. Of course, there was a lot of whispering around the town about the meeting of the classes. It was the biggest event that had taken place since the revolt, and people were suddenly filled with hope.

But hope is contagious, and the government's agents needed to stop what our hero was planning to do. Chris Winterson had approached Wu Lin right after the meeting to ask if she was going to convey the news to the higher authorities, but she seemed quite confused. She was not sure if that was something she should do because of the chip that was altering her decisional capacities.

Chris found it surprising that she said no because Wu Lin had better connections in the government than him. Normally, she would be the first one to communicate any suspicious activities to them. Now, a person had just announced that he was planning on undermining the entire government, and Wu Lin did not care?

All of a sudden, it hit him: *Is Wu Lin in on it?*

He was not sure yet, but he had to be sure before he could go to the authorities. Any wrong or misleading information on such a sensitive topic could quite easily get him executed. He needed to tread lightly and yet, quickly to find the underlying cause of the matter. . . Just then, Damian walks up to Chris. "Chris, great to see you. Thanks so much for coming. Cutting edge stuff, heh? Here, let's toast to our success. Damian hands Chris a glass of champagne to toast. Both men raised their glasses and guzzled the Roederer Champagne. Damian then excused himself. "Excuse me, Chris, I have hosting duties. We'll talk later."

Meanwhile, our hero and his four friends were working actively on finalizing their preparations for the plan to be implemented. While

Wilgred had identified all the legal and technical boundaries that they might need to break in order to achieve their purpose, Aelio and Arctay were proofing their plan for any miscalculations or shortcomings. This had to be the perfect plan. Nothing like this was ever done before, and if even the tiniest fraction of a calculation was to go wrong, it would impact not only the chip's functionality but also their entire future.

"Something's up, I tell you. Ever since the meeting of the classes, I feel like something's cooking elsewhere, too...." JW said while they were all in Damian's conference room.

"What do you mean, JW? What could it be?" Our hero asked, intrigued to know whatever there was to know so that they could handle the situation.

"There were many people at the meeting... What if someone leaks the news?" He asked his fellow men. And what was up with you talking to Chris Winterson, D? Damian confuses him with only a wry smile.

"Well, then we'll deal with it," Said Aelio, unchallenged and not at all bothered by any obstacles. "I mean, if something goes wrong, we'll make it right. That's the only way forward, isn't it?"

"No, Aelio... JW is right... I hope nothing goes wrong, but if JW is expecting trouble, we all know that trouble is on its way. Of course, we will deal with it, but we need to be prepared in time before something bad happens and things go out of control," our hero confessed.

"It's true... Nothing of this sort has ever been done before, and now we're doing it on such a huge level that if we get caught, we are done for our lives. They won't even arrest us – they'll just shoot us." Wilgred was suddenly concerned and thinking hard of ways that they could get past this.

"But first, we need to identify the root causes of any trouble that may arise. For instance, who do we suspect to leak the information about our plan?" Arctay, our hero's younger brother, asked the group.

Damian watched as the four men sat in silence, lost in thoughts, saying nothing as a storm of possible situations overtook their minds. This was not an ordinary mission, and these were not ordinary people. Their intentions, especially now that they were public, made them either heroes or criminals in the view of the public. But they knew who they were among themselves, and they knew that their fight was for the betterment of their country. They were the new army for the common people because the armed military was already brought by the governmental authorities to serve them and only their purposes.

"Are you sure that the meeting of the classes was the right thing to do?" Wilgred asked. "We could have done this without letting them know, you know... It would have been safer...."

"No, Wilgred. I know that you are concerned for our safety right now, but it would not have been right to make decisions for the people without their knowledge. We're doing this for them, right? And... we needed the financial assistance as well. We need to make several more chips, still, and that would have been impossible without the investment that the meeting's Class 1 attendees provided us with."

"Well, that's true, too, but if the cat is out of the bag, Damian, I tell you, we're doomed," He shook his head, worried.x

"Don't worry, gentlemen" Damian says after listening to his compadres. I must now reveal something to you all that had to be timed just right. I put a chip into Wu to ensure she would not betray us. I also set up surveillance on her at the meeting. Only one person made contact with her. Chris Winterson. The reason we had each guest leave all devices capable of transmitting at the door was to ensure no communications were made at the meeting. You asked me why I was talking with Chris? Well, of course, to be the perfect host greeting all the guests. But yes, you know me and after listening to their conversation, I knew I had to act. I put a chip in good ol' Mr.

Winterson's very expensive champagne drink. Needless to say, he will not be a problem." "D, where does it stop? I mean, how do we know who to chip and when is enough", asked Wilgred.

"We have picked the right battle, my fellow men. Don't you worry. If the worst takes its toll, I will take responsibility for all of this and face whatever they put me through, but in the meantime, I will need all of you to continue the plan. I'm ready to pay the price of this idea with anything, including my life, but the plan must not stop. As it happened, I had planned for a few to stand out at the meeting. I am just glad it was only two. I know what a powerful weapon we have here and I know that together, we can succeed. No more secrets, We have come too far to stop. We cannot dangle the dream in front of all these people and then take it away." Damian said conclusively.

His friends gave him protesting looks, but his expression told them that this was the definitive answer anyway.

"We're all in this together, Damian. We'll deal with whatever comes, but for now, we're going to keep going with the execution of our plan," Aelio emphasized, and they all nodded in agreement.

"Grandfather, I have a question," Etha raised her hand. "What did our heroes mean by picking the right battle? How do we know if we picked the right battle?" She asked a very good question, and it instantly reminded me of another story that the children would love...

Let me tell you, kids, a story about a conflict I had. There was this kid, Reggie, who was good-looking and thought the world owed him just for who he was. I think he thought more of himself than others did. I have told you many times that I do not like to fight. It does not mean that I cannot fight, though. One should never mistake someone's decency or morality as their weakness because, in fact, someone who is in control of their emotions and instincts is actually a stronger person than someone who would pounce into a fight the first chance they get.

I do insist that, whenever possible, one should prevent or avoid fighting. Pick your battles, guys, at least when you can. Sometimes you will fight out of necessity – for instance, when someone tries to wrongly take what is yours, don't let them get away with it. Don't be suppressed because even accepting humiliation can be a form of self-harm. So, when someone tries to oppress you— fight time!

But, again, don't do it unless you have to. If a conflict can be resolved through communication, i.e., *verbal* communication, my dear grandchildren, that is the way of adults. That is the most mature way to handle a conflict instead of jumping into a fight.

However, there may be times when you do not feel like words, or verbal communication is enough to resolve a conflict. For instance, if someone keeps bullying you, you can only warn them for so long before you puff up your chest and stand tall against their height. So, this is where your mental capability and decision making skills enter the picture – you have to choose whether your talents and abilities to resolve the situation peacefully are efficient at the right time given all the circumstances, and then, you must be able to recognize when there is a need to put up a fight because let's face it: some people just do not understand the language of peace until a punch tells them what you mean! Ha!

"So, did you ever punch someone, Grandfather?" One of the kids surrounding me chimed in, curious to know more about their grandfather's action-filled adventures.

Well… There was this one time when I was about 13 years old. I will tell you this story to emphasize that one must not fight until one has to, and how you, as kids, can also identify situations of conflict and act accordingly. So, we were newly teenage kids just playing outside around the block.

You see, kids, nowadays, you see that the streets and the parks are nearly empty. There is hardly any life left outside, and we all stay tied up with our electronic screens in our houses, forgetting to appreciate the sun, the sky, the stars. But, when I was a kid, the neighborhoods were full of kids who played out in the streets. Of course, I was one of those kids, too. In fact, in two of our streets, there were no less than fifty kids playing around, all aged between six to fifteen years old!

"Wow…" One of the grandkids said in wonder as he imagined the streets full of kids running around.

We had a lot of fun as kids, my dears. It was really a time to be remembered and missed and talked about. I had many playmates in that old neighborhood, and well, one summer day, I suppose that kid that I was talking about earlier…

"Who, Reggie?" One of the little twins immediately recalled.

"Yes. That kid. Reggie." I nodded, glad that the kids were listening carefully to all that I was saying.

So, I guess this kid, Reggie Yeargin, was having a dreadful day, or maybe he was just that way. I don't know – there was something strange about that boy, especially when he was in a bad mood. He was a good kid to play with, but no one liked even being around him when he was having a dreadful day. He was just a really mean kid who would always be going around blaming the world for his own problems.

Well, now that I have grown up to see many kids like yourselves, I now realize that despite his mean nature, this attribute of whining about his problems and holding the world responsible for it is nothing strange for a kid, really. I mean, this is what almost all kids do. Maybe I used to, too, but I don't know. My elders could comment better on that.

Anyways, it really annoyed me that the other kids were actually afraid of this Reggie kid. He was one of the older kids in the streets in our neighborhood – I suppose he was around 15 at the time when I was 13, and him being a few years older than most other kids there made him feel like he was somehow superior to us. In other words, he tried to tell the other kids around, dominate them, and kind of bully them, as was his reputation. Other kids usually steered clear of him to avoid any conflicts, but I was not afraid of him. I just avoided him to avoid unnecessary drama.

However, this one summer day, I suppose Reggie was determined to project his anger on the first person he sees just because he was in a snit about something. I'll go on with the story, my kids, but let me tell you something interesting before that: we all have different mechanisms built into our brains, and that is how we operate through life. Most people who I have encountered seemed to have projection as their major defense mechanism. Through this, people project their negative feelings like anger and hatred towards other people who may have nothing to do with how that person feels. So, many times you will see that one conflict can lead to several conflicts with other people if you keep projecting your anger in the wrong direction.

Anyways, so Reggie was just trying to find a victim to project his anger on that day. Unfortunately, I was the first person available to him that day. During a conversation, I said something that probably triggered him or something. I don't know exactly what I said that bothered him, but anyway, I said something that he did not like, and it gave him the excuse he needed to direct his anger at me.

I was just standing there talking to him or someone else when he approached me and shoved me! I was nearly knocked down, and I stared back at him, shocked, as he shouted some unintelligible expressions at me. Now, I was not like the other kids who would go sulk in a corner after something like this. Dear grandchildren, your grandfather has never taken crap from anyone! Pardon my language, but you are all old enough now to understand what I mean. I was never someone who would let any unjust behavior go unanswered.

To make it worse, I had a nasty temper in those days, too. Normally, I can predict when things are about to get heated up, so I would have walked away with my tail between my legs long before he could have gotten up to me had I seen this coming. But I was already having a difficult day even before this incident happened. I was distracted by my own day's thoughts to actually think this through.

And, hey, the reason I would have walked away earlier before the conflict could arise was not at all because this Reggie guy scared me, or was two years older than me, bigger than me, or more popular than I was. I would have walked away because I was smarter than him and would rather not get tangled up in a useless fight. No, I was scared of myself!

So, when he shoved me out of the blue, I knew that this was it. My difficult day had reached its limit, and the time to walk away had long gone, so there was only one thing to do as I stared back at him with rage in my eyes: Fight. Honestly, though, if he had looked at my eyes a few moments before he made that stupid move to shove me, he would have known better than to tangle with me.

I quickly got my stance and prepared for a battle. By this time, several other kids had gathered around us to see what was going on. They had left their balls, left their toys and bikes, left their gossips, and came running to stand in the forming circle around us to see what was going to happen next. Generally, if it were any other kid on the ground against Reggie, they would have expected Reggie to win the battle for the bully that he was. But it was me, and I was not about to get bullied by this little boy who thought he could get away with anything. I realized that if he could project his anger at me, I could very well turn him into my punching bag, too.

Experiences kicked in, and instinct took over as I began wailing a torrid horde of blows upon him, each one more devastating than its predecessor.

"Grandfather! You have such a habit of using fancy words. Why don't you just make it easier for us and say that you kicked his ass?! What is this *torrid horde of blows?!*" An annoyed little grandkid wailed.

"Well, I could, if I wanted to... but as you said, I have a way with words, and instead of making it easier, I am going to continue having my way with words."

Everyone chuckled.

"What happened then, Grandpa?" A curious little one asked, wanting to know how the story unfolds.

Oh... Hold your horses, boy.

What happened next was that the bully could not believe that someone stood up to him. To *him*! It was a complete shock for not only Reggie but also the other kids watching the show. I could see it on Reggie's face that he was already regretting tangling up with me in the first place. Clearly, no one had ever stood up to him, let alone fight back or hit him! And I, on the other hand, had landed some pretty impressive punches on that shocked kid.

Now, the lesson is this, my grandkids, that there is a fine line between standing up for yourself and fighting. What Reggie did was unfair, and that is what fighting is, which is obviously not a good thing to do. It could end very badly for you like it did for him. What I did that day was what you would call standing up for yourself. Being your grandpa, I want to teach you, my dear grandchildren, to never let anyone use you, abuse you, or exploit your rights. Your own personality should be so strongly built that you would know how to react in the given circumstances when such a conflict arises.

So, anyway, Reggie had learned his lesson. As soon as I had fought back with him, he realized that all this time, his bark was much worse than his bite, and he quickly gave up. He retreated in his steps, signaling that the fight was over, and as the crowd of kids, some pre-teens and some teenagers, dispersed, we eventually talked and resolved our differences.

You know, there was another thing that was interesting about the fight that contributed to how Reggie quickly gave up. Do any of you know what it was?

"You punched him really hard?" The circle of kids gathered around started to chuckle at the remark.

Well, kind of, but no, not that. I didn't hit him that hard, to be honest. But the thing that made him give up almost immediately and made him realize his mistake was the element of surprise. Being a regular bully, Reggie could not even imagine that any of his preys would stand up to him, let alone fight him off. So, when I did that, he was surprised. I did something that he was not expecting even the slightest bit, and that made him stop and think about what he did. So, I guess, sometimes the element of surprise can be amazingly effective in dealing with conflicts.

As for me, I was prepared. Remember, my dear grandchildren, that preparation is particularly important to deal with any conflict, whether it is verbal or physical. In my case with Reggie, my preparation came from my experience of having a hot temper as well as being able to react to any situation. And, of course, the element of surprise that came from the proper prompting resulted in a more effective resolution of the conflict. And, most of all, the confidence that I had in my physical response to Reggie's attack came from my wrestling and taekwondo training in school, so that was a great add-on!

"Whoa, Grandfather! You knew wrestling even back then?!" A surprised monologue was heard.

"Um, yeah. You guys know I was a state champion in wrestling, right?"

"Yes, grandfather," Said one of the girls. "And I especially like hearing about the time you were competing for the state championship when there was this one match in which no one could tell who was going to win from the holds you two had each other in! And then, 1… 2… 3… you won!"

"Uh… Good one, kid, but I see that you have taken to heart that old phrase, 'stop me if you have heard this one…'. Right?"

There was a crowd of laughter from the group of grandkids sitting around their grandfather.

"Yeah… I know… Your grandfather can get very repetitive about some stories but, it is just that… it was an incredibly special time for me," I said a bit feebly, belying my normally stoic presence. Umph, So this is what helped our heroes decide on their battle. Sometimes one is drawn into battle.

But, my dear grandchildren, I mention these things to bring out a point and teach you a lesson. Each one of my anecdotes and stories has a lesson for you in them if you listen to them carefully and remember them by heart.

You know, my children, this story about Reggie and our conflict that I just told you holds one important lesson: Standing up for what is right. Now, in life, you will grow up to see many people suffering through injustice, many people doing wrong to others, and then many people trying to serve humanity in one way or another. Regardless, we are all brought into this world with our unique purposes. For some, they live to fix the wrongs in the world, while others fight to make way for their own causes. Still others simply give up. They give up because they have no hope. No hope that things can improve.

There is nothing wrong with being in a battle – in fact, having something to fight for is what gives your life purpose and motivation, but what battles you pick determine how worthy your fight is.

Sometimes, as I said before, you can be drawn into battle or a fight. Other times you can join a battle. Avoid starting a battle.

In some instances, you have little choice. But I recommend walking away whenever possible. There are causes ranging from supporting endangered species to the dream of equal rights for everyone to joining a misguided group whose sole criteria for admission is the comparison of their skin tone to a brown paper bag! I mean, can you imagine?!

"What is that about, Grandfather?" Rahij asked, curious at the way I had said the last sentence.

"Well, for some time when I was younger, there was a group of women in a very exclusive club who had put up a very strange fight. These were bright, beautiful, brilliant, and ambitious ladies who engineered Pete Rose's entry into the hall of fame for his accomplishments... Anyway, that is a long and irrelevant story. What I am trying to tell you is that you should have a passion for fighting for a cause that you honestly believe in. That is the right fight for you, and that is the one that you should pick."

For instance, take our hero, Damian. He had a cause to fight for, too. Despite the moral dilemma, he knew that he had to save the people from the unjust acts of the government and the powerful authorities. I remember a phrase from olden literature that says:

"Love your neighbor as you love yourself."

Our hero was to embark on a mission that was the right fight for him – the fight that was likely to present several conflicts, but our hero knew that he was determined to achieve the bigger cause in spite of any obstacles. What better way to show your love than to be willing to die for your beliefs/ Too many lives were at stake to even consider any other course of action, and he knew that nothing else had worked to ease the tensions that were felt everywhere.

CHAPTER 11
A GLITCH

Is everyone enjoying our little get-together here so far?

"Yes!" Roared the group of grandchildren.

"But, grandfather, how does the story end? What happens to our hero's plan?" Rahij asked excitedly, tired of the long lecture his grandfather had given about moral dilemmas and choosing your battles.

"Steady, boy, we're getting there."

So, my dear grandchildren, once the big meeting of the classes was over and the plan was set in motion, our hero asked his partners, or our side-heroes, if they had any questions.

"What about future targets? And what do we do now to keep the Feds off our case?" Arctay asked as the men made their way back into the huge conference room.

"Well, as you know, we have masked our copyrights, patents, and permits with very generic language… Uh, Wilgred? Are we straight on the patents yet?" Our hero asked to confirm before he could go on.

"Absolutely," he quickly and confidently states.

"The trick is not to be greedy in trying to market the smaller chip. We keep it to ourselves. We do not mass-produce the chips. We use our 4D printer to produce the chips. We control everything. The site, the timing, everything. With our extensive lobbying efforts, though, it will simply seem like they got to him with no indication of anything irregular. As for other targets, we need to look at the ecommerce giants and the social media giants next. Their employee conditions are horrible, and they show no concern for them. They deny breaks or family leave, require an inordinate amount of overtime. They make it exceedingly difficult for work-life balance. The worst of it is they do not pay their employees livable wages. They needed to consider their plan of action very carefully to determine exactly what the end game would be for these leeches."

After that, the revolt occurred… I have already told you about that in detail, haven't I?

"Yes, Grandfather!" Elihu chimed. Uh… I forgot…

Anyway, um, the meeting was a success. The new revolt occurred, and in the meantime, something *was* cooking up as they had expected.

"What, grandfather? Did someone rat them out?" Marisol asked with curiosity beaming in her shiny eyes.

"Unfortunately… Yes."

There was a man named Luther Adams. A man Damian always suspected of treachery. Apparently, he had informed a police officer about our activities.

"Oh, no!" The grandchildren looked worried, knowing that our hero was in danger now.

"What, then, grandfather?!" Elihu asked, concerned.

"Well, our hero believed that nothing of immense value can be achieved without struggle, and no good story can be concluded without a conflict… So, let's just say that our hero was expecting this to happen. In fact, he had already played every situation out in his mind before he revealed his plan at the meeting of the classes and was now only waiting for the rest of the events to take place as he imagined.

One day, while he was standing in his garden by the fence, a police vehicle stopped in front of his house. They came up to him and confirmed his name before asking him, politely, to be seated in their car. He knew that it was the procedure, and there was no use rebelling against the situation at hand, so he obeyed. It was best for him to obey, honestly, because, my dear grandchildren, as I mentioned, Damian was a very calculating man.

This is so important, my dear children, because I want you all also to be aware of when to show power or authority and when to obey in silence. This wisdom and ability to judge situations comes with experience, but it is an important life lesson to calculate risks before taking any step. Many people make the mistake of acting too violently or aggressively in situations that require patience. They end up aggravating the situation and complicating things for themselves. So, as we go on with the story, keep this little lesson with you in your pockets, alright, little ones?

"Yes, grandfather!"

Okay, so where were we? Ah, yes: Damian was a very calculating man, and as he was being escorted in handcuffs to the police vehicle, he did not try to fight them off. Once they had arrived at the police station, he was told that there were several leads that made him the prime suspect… but something very unexpected happened.

The police did not accuse him of trying to overturn the government or for cooking up propaganda against the authorities. Instead, they accused him of the absolutely unimaginable: "You are under arrest for the murder of your wife, Rose, and for the terrorist attack on the Main Church street."

Damian looked at them in amazement. *What?!*

He had not expected such an accusation, but he understood that this was all a setup. They had no evidence to prove that he was in on the conspiracy against the government yet, but they could easily manipulate proof to imprison him as a murderer or terrorist for a long time.

Our hero demanded that he wanted to get in touch with his lawyer, and can anyone guess who his lawyer was?

D3 raised his hand excitedly. "Wilgred, grandfather! Wilgred was his lawyer!"

Yes, very good, Damian! Wilgred immediately arrived at the police station to bail him out, but before he could leave, one of the highest-ranked police officers came out to smoke a cigarette and approached Damian and Wilgred with a threatening expression. The next day, Wilgred would take the documentation Damian had prepared for just such a time. He would quickly have the charges dismissed.

"You better watch your steps, Damian. You're playing in deep, muddy waters." He said, blowing the smoke in our hero's face. Feeling dishonored, our hero took the cigarette from the officer's hand and threw it to the cemented ground, crushing it under his shoe.

"It's strange, officer, that you see that warning on the cigarette's packet and still smoke it. It's not good for you, you know, and when something is not good for you, it should be cut out and crushed just like that. That's exactly what I'm doing in the muddy waters, officer. Crushing what's not good for us…." Our hero said with humor and walked away. The officer's face was scrunched up in anger. No one had ever treated him like that.

The children laughed. They felt happy that the hero was able to stand courageously and get away from there, but unfortunately, getting bail was not the way out for our hero. He knew that they would come for him again, and this time, they would not need a legal procedure to disarm or harm him. Sure, Wilgred easily got the charges dismissed. It was the inconvenience and the message Damian perceived that gave him pause.

"From now on, Damian, always have one of us by your side," Wilgred advised. "I may have the law in my hand, but they are not going to work according to the law anymore. You know that."

"I'm not a coward, Wilgred, but yes, one of you can choose to stay with me if that is what you advise. However, we must pace up. Our plan cannot wait anymore."

Our hero had already called a meeting in his massive conference room with the giant table and the tall chairs while he was on his way home with Wilgred. The other three men of the group arrived in time, too, and as the five men sat at the table, they knew it was time to do or die.

"Our plan is already in place, Damian," Aelio pointed out to assure him, "The first stage of our plan's execution was done well under your supervision. As we had intended, we have already put the chip into the Senator, and that has begun the chain reaction. The vote was in our favor. And, as of now, there's a great conflict among the politicians as one of them has voted in the public's favor. That was very unexpected of a man like him, you know."

"Yes, and now, that has made the other politicians rethink their stance and question what is going on within the parliament so that their focus is away from us at the time," Arctay included.

"Well, that is just perfect, then. Now, we have more time to actively implant our chips into more politicians and kickstart our *Pow-Wow* plan!" Our hero cheered.

Despite the trouble, he knew he was in, he was happy that his mission was not compromised. You see, my dear grandchildren, that is the essence of a good life: you must not get demotivated or scared away by obstacles. Obstacles are a part of life. If anything, our hero believed that obstacles in his path only made the journey more interesting. Don't you think?

The group of grandchildren smiled widely.

"Yes, grandpa. Like, the obstacle in our hero's mission has made the story more interesting," Elihu chimed.

Exactly. So, whenever something goes wrong in your life, always tell yourself, '*Okay, it is about to get more interesting now!*'

Of course, our hero was planning to overturn the entire government, and that was not as easy as he made it sound. It was his optimism that allowed him to even believe in his plan. Otherwise, it was really a miracle that they were still alive after their plan was out.

Soon after the meeting was over, the four friends of our hero left the conference room with separate roles assigned to each one of them. Arctay had volunteered to stay at Damian's house to ensure that he is protected at all times. After all, he was his brother, and even though the others had wanted to stay, too, Damian deemed it appropriate for his brother to stay by his side.

Once the other men had left our hero's house, Arctay and Damian sat in the lounge wondering what they could do if there was an intrusion in the house or if the police came for them again.

"At this point, Damian, the only reaction that I see fit is that you flee the scene. If they find you, I am sure that they will not let go easily," he said.

"Yes, Arctay, you're right. I won't flee, but I can hide. We will have to use our bunker/basement, built just for this purpose." He stated.

Rose was no longer in his house, and ever since her death, Damian had embraced the loneliness of the huge house. Now that he was in trouble, however, he realized that this loneliness was, indeed, a blessing. He had no one there to protect and no one to fear losing. He had already communicated to his children to not visit him for a few weeks saying that he was on a mission and had already bid farewell to his grandchildren, leaving their innocent minds to wander, thinking what their grandfather's mission could be.

Meanwhile, our hero's younger brother had decided that he would not even hesitate to sacrifice his own life to save his brother's, our hero's life. He had been brainstorming for ways to keep Damian safe in case the police or any other people broke into their house to *arrest* him again.

"We use the hidden basement?" He suggested that night at dinner. They were having beef steaks with some cheese sauce. There was silence for a while – no sound other than the clinking of their forks and knives against their plates.

Our hero was not selfish; he could not feel comfortable with the plan even though he had agreed on it earlier. If he would hide, they would take away his brother instead. They just needed a prey and Damian knew well what they were capable of doing to their catch.

"If I hide, you hide, too. Okay?" He finally said, feeling Arctay's eyes on him.

Arctay smiled, knowing what was bothering our hero.

"Damian, I believe in you and your purpose. Your leadership is vital to the success of our mission – our mission to save humanity. I am not offering my life's sacrifice to save only yours. No…" He paused, and then hung his head low as if to hide any trace of fear evident in his eyes. He finds the courage and says, "No, I am doing whatever I am doing for our mission. If humanity can be saved by my sacrifice, I would not think twice about it."

Damian was not an emotional person. He was a wise man with a strong heart, but hearing this from his younger brother wetted his eyes.

"Let's go to the basement tomorrow. Then we can decide who sacrifices and when…" Damian was impressed by the brave exterior put on by Arctay. He always knew that his brother held great potential, but to offer one's life is the greatest form of love one can give.

After they were done with dinner, the two brothers took a round each around the house, inspecting every possible way to conceal their little hideout while evaluating how easy or difficult it would be for the cops or anyone else to locate it. Of course, they needed a place best hidden from the eyes of a stranger entering the house. Most people were not aware of the basement in Damian's home. They used this to their advantage.

They knew that since the secret of their activities was out and Damian had shown himself to be representing and leading the mission, the Feds would not let him off the hook so easily. They will come again. They will try to hurt him, and this time, God knows what they were going to use against him.

"The arrest was a warning, Damian," Arctay finally said. "It won't be a warning this time, you know that, right?"

Damian knew that, and he nodded. But, he was not too worried for himself. He had done what he needed to do and achieved what he needed to achieve in his life. He had loved his wife immensely and had done his best to give her a wonderful life. He had raised his children with love and with wisdom, making them all good family men and women. He had seen his grandchildren laugh and cry. What more could a man want from his life?

Yet… He knew that none of those things equaled his need to make his *Pow Wow* mission work. Arctay was right: his survival was vital to the success of his mission, and that is why he had to continue living. He had to protect himself at any and all costs.

After the brothers had inspected the house, Damian suggested they go home. Damian's mansion came complete with its own secret basement and tunnel system. It had a long tunnel underground, leading to the garden outside. He was always thinking ahead

Arctay was always impressed with all that his brother had accomplished. "Sounds like the only idea to me. We use the tunnel as an escape route if the need arises. What do you say?"

"I say, let's do it," Our hero said as they continued preparing. Once they were done, the two men knew that this would only be the beginning.

The basement was as lavish as the rest of the house. Once they were satisfied with the hiding place, they returned to the main house and carefully replaced the carpet and rugs back as neatly as they had taken them off. The carpet blended in well with the other settings of the lounge, making it look homely. No one could suspect a thing about this basement.

The sun was up, and the rays of sunshine entering through the windows making the drops of perspiration on our heroes' foreheads glimmer. They had made it through the night safely.

They both laughed, reflecting on it. In the meantime, instructions had already been given to the other side heroes in our story, and they were actively fulfilling their duties, planting the tiny chips into the people of the government. Things were about to change.

CHAPTER 12
TURNING THE TABLES

Arctay and Damian had not had much sleep last night, so they decided to nap during the day. However, a loud thud startled Arctay as he woke up, looking around to see no sign of Damian. He ran quickly to the bedroom where Damian usually slept, and he was not there either. *Shit!* Arctay was worried now. "Grandfather, language! Rowena reminds. "Yes, dear," he replies.

Arctay started to run around the house looking for Damian but could not find him anywhere. However, when he entered the lounge, he saw two masked men aiming rifles at him.

"Stay where you are!"

"Knees on the ground and hands on your head!"

They yelled, and Arctay obeyed. He knew better than to cause trouble around them. They would not even blink before shooting him, and Arctay needed to know that Damian was okay before that could happen.

"Grandfather?" Elihu asked innocently.

"Yes, dear?"

"Did our heroes have no superpowers or guns?" She asked, curious as to why our heroes were not kicking the bad guys' asses already.

My dear little girl, you remember what I told you children about knowing how and when to pick your battles, right? Our hero, Damian, and our side-heroes were all very well equipped with the power of intelligence and wit. They had guns, yes, but only for the protection of each other and their beloved – not to make an impact in any other way. They knew that it was better and smarter to deal with such issues without violence, because my dear children, violence begets violence. Bloodshed is never the answer.

"But, grandfather, what if they kill our heroes with their guns? Their brains won't be so useful, then, right?" asked Mequella.

I laughed. Of course not, my dear impatient grandchildren!

"But, grandfather! Continue the story! Where is Damian? Is he hiding?" Nubia asked.

Ah, yes! Damian... Our hero was quick and smart. He had heard the alarm too late and realized that they had not considered one very important thing about the hideout they chose. They did not realize that if the alarm system fails and someone breaks into the house through the front door, they enter the lounge directly, and that made it impossible for Damian to go through there. Instead, our hero had jumped out of his bedroom's window into the garden and... Can anyone guess what he must have done?

"Yes, grandfather! Either he ran away, or he went into the long tunnel they had in place that opened in the garden!" One of the twins chanted delightfully.

Very good! Yes, he had used the escape opening to enter the tunnel and had traveled through it to the bunker where he had originally planned to hide. Isn't that smart?

"Yes, grandfather!"

But, he wasn't just smart; he was armed, too. Before he had climbed down into the tunnel, he had unpinned and thrown a grenade near the unfamiliar car parked in front of his house. It was the intruder's car and had Feds' license plate. But what he did not know was that Luther Adams, a man he had long suspected of treachery, had ratted him out and was hiding in that car's backseat.

He was curious to know what Damian would be put through. He was generally very envious of Damian because of the respect he had earned. People did not treat Luther the same way because he had been known as a snitch or as a selfish man, so when he did not get respect from people, he decided to try and get it from the Feds by feeding them with the information they wanted.

When the explosive sound successfully diverted the intruders' attention away towards the outside, they forgot about Arctay to quickly run out of the house, trying to catch a glimpse of Damian. They had orders from the Feds to kill Damian as soon as he was seen, and their rifles were locked and loaded to do just that. They saw a man, a shadowy figure, moving around at their car's backseat and immediately presumed that he was their prey, Damian.

Now, my dear grandchildren, before I proceed, I want to give you a very important lesson. Life is unfair at times; yes, it is true; but, life is also fair when it comes to giving people what they deserve. Have you ever heard of the term 'karma'?

"Yes, grandfather, but we don't know what it means…"

Okay, then, I think we should understand karma before continuing the story. How many of you have gotten a good beating after doing something your parents told you not to do?

The grandchildren raised their arms, embarrassed.

Haha! Impressive! You are all little rebels, aren't you? Okay, so now, think of fate as your parents. When you do something bad, fate punishes you in one way or another. If you steal something, something will get stolen from you. If you hurt someone, you will get hurt, too. And, karma is not just for bad actions – there is good karma, too. If you help someone in need, you will be helped when you are in trouble, too. So, whatever you do in life, you get a reward or punishment for it in a just and fair way. Do you all understand?

"Yes, grandfather!" The children said in unison.

All right. Always remember to do good by others, my dear grandchildren. A life worth living is one in which you are useful for others, good to others, and are valued by others. Now, that does not mean that your true worth and value are always decided by what others think of you. No, don't get me wrong, kiddos, but what I am saying is that you gain respect when you are good to others, and that increases your true value.

Whenever you will help people, you know what you will become? Heroes! You will become their hero for that day or for that time, and whenever they will think of you or see you, they will be genuinely delighted. Being a hero is really as simple as that, my kids. Just be good to people.

Now, back to the story. Where were we?

"The Feds had seen Damian in the car!"

Uh… no, no. They weren't the Feds; they were people, more likely gangsters, hired by the Feds to kill Damian. And that wasn't Damian in the car… It was Luther Adams! I told you guys that he had climbed into their car, right? This time annoyed that they were *not* listening.

So, the two armed men had no idea that anyone other than Damian could have reason to approach their car. They thought that Damian had sneaked out of the house and was trying to escape in their car, so they instantly started to fire shots aimed at him. They kept shooting until all the bullets in their chambers were out, and that is when Arctay and Damian came running out of the house and shot them both.

I should not be telling you kids about such violent stories, and I am sure that your moms are going to be pretty mad at me later, but well, what's a story without some action, eh?

The kids laughed and then became quiet, waiting for their grandfather to continue telling the story. It had gotten intense for them.

Well, the Feds' gangsters had been taken by surprise. They worked according to their basic intuition while our heroes combined their intuitive capacities with their intelligent thinking and devised a quick plan. With just two shots and a grenade, they had gotten rid of the two intruders who were most likely murderers, and even without their intention to do so, those murderers had shot at least seven bullets through Luther's body that lay lifeless in their car's backseat then.

A few neighbors had gathered after the final gunshots were heard, and they were terrified. However, they knew that the Feds were behind this attack on Damian and his friends, and they did not blame him for killing them. Amidst the chaos, Wu Lin came forward and peeked into the enemy's car to see Luther lying on the bloody seat.

"Got him right!" She said to Damian.

Damian and Arctay were not even aware that there was a dead body in the enemy's car until then. They had just distracted the two killers with a grenade and then shot them from behind, and so far, they were thinking that the killers were shooting blindly. But, when Wu Lin stated this fact, Damian and Arctay quickly took a look at Luther, and their faces turned pale.

"Well, it is done…." Damian said, looking downward, shaking his head, relieved that he had not killed an innocent person. Luther did not die from his bullets, but he had caused the distraction that attracted the killers towards him, so he could not help but feel relieved that it was Luther and not him.

"You did the right thing. He deserved it!" Wu Lin said again, trying to cheer Damian up. She had a newfound respect for him not only because of the chip, but also because her newer thoughts had altogether changed her nature: she was a kinder, fairer person now.

"Wait, what? Why did he deserve it? He was our neighbor…" Arctay began to say but then trailed off, realizing that this man was actually in the enemy's car.

"Don't you know? He was the one who told the Feds about your activities. His smug ass always hated Damian… He asked me to partner with him to prove you guys guilty, too. I said no, so he tried to do it on his own," She explained before going towards Damian who again was a little relieved knowing that he had killed a man of the enemy, not an innocent one.

"You're doing a great job, Damian. I'm so glad you're okay," She brushed his arm with her hand gently before walking away. The rest of the neighbors had also started going away back into their houses while our heroes cleaned up their garden.

The other three fellows of our hero were also called and they buried the dead bodies in a graveyard nearby.

CHAPTER 13
HAPPINESS

When the rest of the team arrived, they hugged Damian, happy to see him alive and fit.

"What's the update on the tasks assigned to you, men?" He asked them without hesitation and without regard for the incidents that had just taken place.

"Well, we're close to our final tasks' completion now, Damian. The entire targeted group of Tiers 2 and 3 of the government officers have been chipped, and we are controlling it all well. Looks like there would be no need to overturn the government anymore. The chip is working just fine to make them work for the public like they should have in the first place." Aelio explained.

Damian smiled, knowing that his mission was succeeding. He knew he had made the difference in the world that he could.

"Now, what about the Feds coming for me again and…." He began to say when Wilgred cut him off.

"No, they won't. That will not happen. Not anymore," His smile told Damian what he meant. "I'm sorry, but I did some things without your authorization…."

That was enough to let the team know what Wilgred had done, and they were all supportive of it. He had implanted the chips into the Lead Investigators for both the FBI and NSA of their areas and district. They were actually a part of their mission now, and instead of causing trouble, they were clearing the ways into the government offices for our heroes.

Our hero was shielding his grandchildren from the day-to-day activities of his ventures. All they knew was that he was a successful writer and investor. They knew enough about his status in the community and the fact that he was greatly respected for his philanthropic work, which he was.

Little did the grandkids know that he was telling his grandchildren about himself. He was Damian, the hero.

In the end, just be who you are, but make sure that who you are is someone worth being. Don't get into fights but fight for your rights and your people when you should. Be strong for not only yourself but also for others.

"Grandfather, what can give a person the right to decide what people think?" asks Kaleb.

That is a super good question! Well, it depends on the situation. The first thing that comes to my mind is the survival of the fittest. Naturally, through acts of nature, the strongest will prevail. Too often, people try to add their own influences in your life or decisions to determine the outcome in their own favor, sometimes intentionally or sometimes subconsciously. In most of these cases, someone else should be involved if for no other purpose than to provide a voice of reasoning.

However, you should care about what other people think only to determine your decisions' moral and ethical logic, nothing more than that. You cannot always care about one's feelings. I am not saying that you should not consider folks' feelings. But there will be times when their feelings conflict with your own purposes. Yes, it is admirable to put someone before yourself. But remember, if you don't take care of yourself, you will not be able to help others. One should be able and willing to achieve their goal by any means necessary regardless of what other people think, as long as the motive is not evil. Because remember, my kids, good will always prevail over evil.

If an act is inherently evil, good will prevail in time. Maybe immediately, or maybe in a thousand years. It is not ours to decide. But, if we have the means and motivation to right a wrong, why should we willingly go by the rules of the ones we are fighting?

Peace by nature, war from compulsion.

"Grandfather... the story you told us today sounds a lot like it is about you... I heard my dad talking a few times about your work when he thought I was asleep. I think you slipped up earlier, too, and said 'I' instead of we, when talking about Damian. Plus, his house sounds like this house, and you have 4 'associate heroes' working with you every day. And then there is Grandmother Rose...Are you the Damian in your story?"

All ears perked up and eagerly awaited my response.

"Hmm..." I said, furthering their curiosity with a smile. Well, my military training would have me respond with, 'I can neither confirm nor deny the information in that area.' However, my time as a federal employee would have me respond truthfully with, 'Yes, I am,' while defending it in a way that you would end up agreeing that there were only *similarities* between the hero and me.

Better yet, my time as a corporate leader would have me consider the political correctness of my response and determine whether you are a friend or a foe before I would formulate an answer. I would think: *Can the information cause damage to me or mine?* And my favorite consideration of all would be: *How much is in it for me?*

So, based on all my experiences and pieces of training, I must be truthful with my grandchildren and say, "Yes."

A long pause hung in the suddenly silent environment.

"And... There are similarities. But this cannot be about me because this story ends... and mine, quite thankfully, has not yet."

"No, Grandpa. This story ends with the success of Damian in reducing the need for further conflict and finding a way to continue efforts to inspire a spirit of unity." One of the smartest kids in the circle pointed out.

"Yes, unity for a cause that benefited those who were deprived for so many years, needlessly and selfishly. And their fight continued. They were able to bring about truly significant change. They continued to upgrade their efforts to block themselves from government exposure. It became a struggle that they managed. And they felt much better about their cause and its chances for success because they had dared to go against the system. A one-sided system that only took and took and took. Viewed by many as heroes. Seen as radical by others. Damian and his crew could no longer sympathize with an uncaring, greedy, maligning government. The change had come at last!

So, what do you think about the story, guys?"

"Um… I don't know yet, Grandfather. Maybe if you could answer some of my questions first… if it is alright?" D3 asked.

"Sure, Damian. Shoot!"

"Okay, so how did you figure out that part about the hackers? I mean, how did this idea come to you, thinking so far outside the box?" His eyes shone with curiosity.

Well, I thought about the talent that it would take to do what I had in mind. I looked at the similarities and differences of each of those major hacks. They each displayed a remarkable knowledge of circuitry, coding, identifying flaws in exploitable vulnerabilities, and gathering information to formulate a plan of attack for their hacks. Their tools allowed them to obtain real-time data. An advantage much appreciated. Their ability to hack Wi-Fi networks was a clincher. It dawned on me that their talents were going to waste, and my idea could help more than harm them.

All I needed to do was to convince them to work with me by being completely honest with them. I appealed to them with the revolt and offered them the chance to make a real difference in the world. They were all politically motivated anyway, so that made the negotiation easier.

Each of them had a cause to believe in, and they were ready to go to extreme lengths to explain or demonstrate their conviction to these causes. So, with my plan, I tasked each of them with altering the dopamine and glutamate levels in the brain of the person who would have the microchip inserted. This way, we could combine the use of their individual efforts to arrive at the best results, namely reversing previous, immutable positions by activating one of the many transistors in the chip. Sounds complicated, I know, but it was the only way.

Now, how that works is that this alteration makes the brain think targeted levels are off. Dopamine levels control the emotional responses one has. Imagine if the brain thought there was not enough or too much dopamine. You'd be a total wreck! Serotonin is also a chemical found in the body. It also regulates mood and emotions. Imagine if your brain thought that there was only, say, 40 % of the required 90+ % of the serotonin in the gut. Your brain would start dumping serotonin into your gut like there was no tomorrow.

That imbalance would cause some serious digestive problems, confusion and before you know it, bad decisions would prevail. Damian's research and consultation with his biologist friend, Dr. Herman Bass, the world's leading authority on chemical reactions involving the brain, helped him fill in some missing pieces, for sure. He met Herman in the First Grade, and they quickly hit it off. Damian always possessed leadership qualities. This is what gave him the edge for the coveted R R Steel award Damian had taken home. Herman had transferred out before that school year began, leaving Damian far less competition. But Herman was one of those guys who are truly brilliant but struggle to teach or even interact on a social level. But Herman, also fascinated by the sciences as a boy, became interested in how the brain functions and became an authority in the field.

Ahh, Damian sighs. The human brain is such a masterpiece in its functionality, and Herman discovered that at a very early age. What we were doing was risky but totally worth it. A good example of how my mind may not operate like others' minds. *Hehe*.

In fact, that is not necessarily a bad thing. We all need the confidence to be who we are. We all need to be brave enough to express who we know we are in our heart of hearts.

"Any other questions or thoughts about the story, fellas?"

"I was wondering, Grandfather... how did you know that somebody won't find out about all of this?" Nubia asked.

"You know, sweetheart, I have no idea! I could only hope that my efforts would be successful because I had no guarantee that it was a safe mission!"

"Yeah, I guess one can take all the precautions they can think of, but something can still go wrong."

It's called Murphy's Law. Dear grandchildren, this very practical law states that anything that can go wrong will go wrong. Hence, one must always be prepared to face any possibility. And that is exactly why I am always telling you guys to as quickly as possible, consider as much as you have available and then make your decision. Sometimes, you will have to decide quickly. Other times, you will have enough time to plan your efforts. Just do your best at all times. A task worth doi-

"-doing is worth doing well!" They all say in unison.

"Yes, Grandfather! We have heard you say this very often!"

Everyone laughs heartily.

"Yeah, yeah! It is just that... I want you guys to remember the importance of taking on tasks that are worthy of your time."

"We love you, Grandfather!"

"And I love you all. Now, let's go see what we can scrounge up to eat, shall we? Who wants barbeque?"

Made in the USA
Las Vegas, NV
16 May 2022

48973800R00085